Mistletoe, Murder, and Mayhem

Sheila Williamson

BookLocker
Trenton, Georgia

Copyright © 2025 Sheila Williamson

Paperback ISBN: 978-1-959624-43-1
Hardcover ISBN: 978-1-959624-44-8
Ebook ISBN: 979-8-88532-111-2

All rights reserved. No part of this publication may be reproduced, stored in a retrieval system, or transmitted in any form or by any means, electronic, mechanical, recording or otherwise, without the prior written permission of the author.

Published by BookLocker.com, Inc., Trenton, Georgia.

The characters and events in this book are fictitious. Any similarity to real persons, living or dead, is coincidental and not intended by the author.

BookLocker.com, Inc.
2025

First Edition

Library of Congress Cataloging in Publication Data
Williamson, Sheila
Mistletoe, Murder, and Mayhem by Sheila Williamson
Library of Congress Control Number: 2025916249

Dedication

This is dedicated to the volunteer Actors of the "Mistletoe, Murder, and Mayhem" screenplay. Thank you: Joann Kahl, Gary Morgan, LeAnn Holt, Nichole Perez, Jesmin Nawaz, Chad Andrus, Jeff Williamson, Mary Greer, Logan Hassinger, Jules Hicks, Mimi Tapia-Bowie, Liz Petit, Kim Tenbrook, Steve Liber, Cyndi Durrance and the best Stage Manager ever, Cyndy Powell

Acknowledgements

This book was such a labor of love for me! It started as a screenplay which I used to fundraise for Meals on Wheels. I recruited many friends for the roles and we all donated our time, talents, and blood, sweat and tears to fundraise. The story came to life. Then came the decision to turn the play into a book. The original play ends when the guests leave The Mistletoe Inn after the killer is revealed. We also made it funny to appeal to the audience.

So…that being said, this would not have happened without those talented actors which I dedicated the book to, as well as my talented son, Chad, who was our incredible sound engineer.

Also, a special thank you to my full time job at Hogue Barnett, PLLC for their unwavered support and some legal expertise with the story.

My husband Jeff, who played Jeff Willingham in the play, helped me with several ideas as well as being a sounding board for my craziness.

I am excited to start this series of mysteries and hope you follow us all over Texas as we explore one place after another.

Sheila

Contents

Prologue: September 5 11
Chapter 1: The Mistletoe Inn 15
Chapter 2: The Owners 19
Chapter 3: Guest Check In 21
Chapter 4: Jeff Willingham, J.D. 29
Chapter 5: Lucille Chambers 31
Chapter 6: The Tree Trimming Party 32
Chapter 7: The Next Day 35
Chapter 8: Dr. Formby 39
Chapter 9: The Investigation 41
Chapter 10: Raven DuPree 46
Chapter 11: Mr. Fathom 52
Chapter 12: More Questions 54
Chapter 13: Scarlett Johnson 58
Chapter 14: Chef Marta 60
Chapter 15: The Scavenger Hunt 62
Chapter 16: The Search Warrant 65
Chapter 17: Guest reactions 70
Chapter 18: Renata Castleberry 72
Chapter 19: Nancy Ellis 74
Chapter 20: Bambi Lynn 76
Chapter 21: Detective Chestnut 78
Chapter 22: The Next Day 79
Chapter 23: The Banquet 82
Chapter 24 A Murderer is Revealed 84

Chapter 25: Guest Reactions 91
Chapter 26: Breakfast 93
Chapter 27: Check Out Time 95
Chapter 28: Jeff Willingham 97
Chapter 29: Detective Chestnut 99
Chapter 30: Staff Plans after Check out 101
Chapter 31: Renata 103
Chapter 32: Caddo Lake 105
Chapter 33: Monday 106
Chapter 34: Live Well Pharmaceuticals 108
Chapter 35: Scarlett's Hearing 112
Chapter 36: The Phone Call 113
Chapter 37 Renata's Disappearance 116
Chapter 38 Renata's Case 118
Chapter 39: Tuesday 120
Chapter 40: The Search Begins 124
Chapter 41: Wednesday in Jeffersonville 126
Chapter 42: Questions and More Questions 129
Chapter 43: Wednesday in Oklahoma City 132
Chapter 44: Thursday in Jeffersonville 135
Chapter 45: Thursday in Oklahoma City 137
Chapter 46: Scarlett's Defense 139
Chapter 47: Jeff Willingham Under Fire 141
Chapter 48: Guests Arrive 145
Chapter 49: Gustav 147
Chapter 50: The Search Begins 150
Chapter 51: Cameron's Quest 152
Chapter 52: Christmas Trivia Night 153

Chapter 53: Saturday 155
Chapter 54: The Ugly Sweater Contest 158
Chapter 55: Police Station 162
Chapter 56: Sunday 165
Chapter 57: Jacksonville Jail 168
Chapter 58: Sunday evening 170
Chapter 59: Scarlett's cell 171
Chapter 60: Monday 172
Chapter 61: The Arraignment 176
Chapter 62: Monday Evening 177
Chapter 63: Tuesday 179
Chapter 64: Sighting 181
Chapter 65: Carols and Cookies 183
Chapter 66: What was Lost was Now Found 186
Chapter 67: Coroner's Office 190
Chapter 68: The Prisoner 193
Chapter 69: Thursday 194
Chapter 70: Friday 197
Chapter 71: The Visit 201
Chapter 72: Sunday 204
Chapter 73: Monday of Christmas Week 207
Chapter 74: Alejandro 211
Chapter 75: Chef Marta 213
Chapter 76: Alejandro's Arraignment 215
Chapter 77: Jeff Willingham 216
Chapter 78: Monday Night 218
Chapter 79: The Dad 219
Chapter 80: Christmas Eve 220

Chapter 81: Christmas Eve at the Prison 222
Chapter 82: Christmas Day 223
Chapter 83: Chef Marta 225
Chapter 84: Christmas in the Jeffersonville Jail 226
Chapter 85: December 26 227
Chapter 86: Oklahoma, Here We Come 229
Chapter 87: A Meeting of the Minds 231
Chapter 88: Jeff Willingham 232
Chapter 89: Chef Marta's Dilemma 234
Chapter 90: Gustav and Olive Learn the Truth 238
Chapter 91: Hands Across the Border 240
Chapter 92: Juan's plan 242
Chapter 93: Juan and Marta Together Again 244
Chapter 94: The Inquisition 245
Chapter 95: New Year's Eve 248
Epilogue 251
About the Author 253

Prologue:
September 5

As Lawyer Jeff Willingham III shuffled paper on his desk, there was a knock at the door. He spoke, "Come in, Mr. Fathom. I have been expecting you. Please take a seat."

Mr. Fathom, a well-dressed, middle-aged man, came in, and took the seat offered to him across the desk from Mr. Willingham. He said, "What is this all about? I don't believe we have met. I currently have no need for an attorney."

Mr. Willingham answered, "Mr. Fathom, as you may or may not know, I represent your uncle, Mr. Cooper, in all his business interests, and his estate as well. He has asked me to have this meeting with you regarding his failing health. In fact, he was placed on hospice care this week and he asked me to convey his last wishes to you as he is not sure how much time he has left."

"I am sorry to hear of this downturn in my uncle's health but I'm still unclear what this immediately has to do with me," said Mr. Fathom.

"Your uncle just recently sold his company to an industry giant and this, added to his already significant wealth, makes him incredibly wealthy. You, Mr. Fathom, are his sole heir." Mr. Willingham paused to let this news sink in, and then continued. "However, your uncle has followed your career quite closely for some time and, for this reason, he has some stipulations on your upcoming inheritance."

Mr. Fathom, genuinely surprised, and feeling more ill at ease by the minute, asked, "What stipulations?"

"Mr. Cooper has given you the task to make things right with five individuals from your past. These individuals are people that you have had bad dealings with over the years. They include a doctor, a young woman who lost both her parents in an accident, two wives, and a best friend of a former employee of yours. Here are the pertinent details." He handed Mr. Fathom a thick file with photos and information inside.

Mr. Fathom, clearly upset and wanting to leave, started to get up from his chair as Mr. Willingham continued, "Now, Mr. Cooper is giving you sixty days to make things right with these people as he recognizes he has made many mistakes in his life, and does not want *you* to be faced with the same regrets in the last years of your life."

Mr. Fathom sighed, and rubbed his head, clearly at a loss for words. Mr. Willingham continued, "I must stress to you the importance of this task and the great reward that will be yours upon completion. You *must* take this seriously as we will be checking. Do I make myself clear?"

Mr. Fathom sighed again, and mumbled, "Yes." He started again to get up from his chair.

Mr. Willingham also stood, and said, "Wait. There is one more thing."

Mr. Fathom, pale and distraught, replied, "What now?"

Mr. Willingham handed him a red envelope. He very carefully opened it to find a gift certificate for a stay at an inn. He explained, "Your uncle knows you will take care of this important task, and wishes to reward you with a stay at The Mistletoe Inn. Everything is all set for a Christmas-themed stay to enhance your Christmas spirit, which will be freed upon you making these things right. Your uncle himself wishes he could join you, but fears he will not be up to it. He wishes *you* to go in his place."

Mr. Fathom started to leave, and shook his head incredulously.

Mr. Willingham said, "Goodbye, Mr. Fathom."

Chapter 1:
The Mistletoe Inn

The owners of The Mistletoe Inn were excited to see the bookings come in for the new Christmas season. They had planned and researched about how to bring in business during the holiday season and it finally was beginning to pay off. This week, from Wednesday through Sunday, they were fully booked! Both Gustav and his wife, Olive, were very excited indeed. This was a first for the inn to be completely full during the week. So, they were holding a special staff meeting with their Chef, Marta, their son, Jackson, who manned the front desk, and the housekeeper, Bambi Lynn, to make sure that everyone was on their toes for these arrivals, and that everything was in place for the upcoming holiday events they had planned.

Gustav, Olive, Marta, Jackson, and Bambi Lynn all gathered in the lobby area with clipboards detailing all the upcoming events, and their particular assignments. Gustav began, "We have a full house beginning this afternoon and we need to all be on the same page to take care of each guest. Tomorrow, after breakfast, the guests will be on their own until 7 p.m. at which time we will have a tree trimming party for them, complete with refreshments and Christmas music. Is everything in place for this event, Chef Marta?"

Chef Marta replied, "Yes. I will be serving hot apple cider and Christmas cookies."

Bambi Lynn joined in, "I will be happy to help Chef with serving the guests. May we also have popcorn and cranberries to string along for the tree? I think the guests might like that."

Chef Marta agreed, "Yes, of course! Great idea. But…may I spike the cider this time?"

Gustav and Olive looked at each other, and agreed. "Yes, that will be fine. Just notify the guests that there is alcohol in case anyone objects. We can serve them plain apple cider, right?"

Chef Marta replied, "Of course. I do not want anyone to be uncomfortable."

Jackson joined in, "I will be sure the Christmas music is on and perfect for the event. But, can we possibly have local entertainer like Charlotte Champion come and share a song or two?"

Gustav heartily agreed and Jackson offered to contact her to see if she could stop by for the event.

Charlotte was known to all the locals as a professional entertainer that appealed to all ages. She was always the go-to when entertainment was needed.

Olive said, "Great! Now, what about the game night planned on Friday? What did you decide? Charades? Board games? Scavenger hunt?"

They all agreed, "scavenger hunt for sure!" Gustav chuckled, and agreed to formulate one for the historic town square. He would make it so the guests checked out all the downtown stores in order to "find" the necessary items for the scavenger hunt. Olive was thrilled, and agreed to transport the guests downtown herself.

Chef Marta asked, "Do we want to have some treats for them when they return?"

Olive agreed and suggested, "What about hot chocolate and smores around the fire pit?"

Chef Marta immediately agreed, and noted that on her list.

Olive then asked, "Should we have a prize for the winner?"

Gustav said, "Already taken care of. Prize bag of several goodies from the square." Everyone agreed to this and then the conversation turned to Saturday evening. That would be the highlight of the weekend, with a fancy dinner and professional entertainment, as promised on the brochure.

Chef Marta started reading off her proposed menu and they all agreed on that as well. She would place her order with the supplier that day.

Gustav cleared his throat, and said, "I have a surprise announcement about the entertainment. Straight from Las Vegas, we have Elvis! Well...an Elvis impersonator anyway and he is supposedly quite good. He had a break in his schedule and he agreed to perform for us! Isn't that fantastic?"

All agreed that this was something completely unexpected and, at the same time, hoped he was as good as people said. Everyone would need to transform the dining room into a holiday banquet, with décor and place settings. They all wanted this event as perfect as possible, resulting in the 5-star reviews they are hoping for. Since the inn had been struggling for a while, all their hopes were riding on those reviews. Reviews are the lifeblood of online bookings and The Mistletoe Inn was seriously in need of more bookings!

Gustav spoke out one more time, "All right, does anyone have any questions? If not, then let's all get started doing everything we can for these guests, and make sure all their stays are simply magical." With that, everyone dispersed, and went on about their day's work.

Jackson formulated an itinerary for each guest, listing all the special events, as well as information about the historic town square, and some other excursion ideas.

Since the guests would have so much free time, Jackson detailed all the things close by that he could think of to entertain them. Nature walks, shopping, wineries, historical landmarks and many more, all within close proximity to the inn.

Later that day, Olive approached Gustav saying, "I am very excited about this weekend. This may be just exactly what we need to put The Mistletoe Inn on the map for good!"

Gustav replied, "I certainly hope so. We cannot go on the way we have been. I'm not sure how much longer we can last without an uptick in bookings. I am trying everything I know to do, Olive, but this may be our last hurrah if it doesn't work." They hugged and Olive tried not to tear up. She knew exactly what Gustav meant. Their finances had been dwindling for some time now. A lot was riding on this first of their holiday-themed weekends but, for it to be a sell out was more than they could have dreamed. She was so hopeful that this is a sign that more good times were coming.

Chapter 2:
The Owners

When Gustav and Olive bought The Mistletoe Inn, they were not experienced innkeepers but they were hopeful entrepreneurs with experience only in the software industry in the northeast. They had dreamed of owning an inn together, and had a vision of being an integral part of the community of Jeffersonville, Texas. They chose Jeffersonville and the inn after a search for a bed and breakfast they could run together. Without experience, they spent time researching what makes a property successful and felt drawn to this property in Jeffersonville, which was in deep East Texas. Not being native Texans, they tried to assimilate as quickly as possible. They joined the local Chamber of Commerce and the downtown merchants' group as they were close in proximity, and wanted to learn about any special events planned there. They renovated, and started advertising, but just could not seem to attract much interest until Gustav's idea about the Christmas-themed stays. All the rooms had been decorated for Christmas, and been individually themed.

They hired a chef and a maid/housekeeper, and their son, Jackson, helped them out at the front desk. Typically, they served breakfast only, and had snacks available for purchase. The inn itself was in fairly good condition, with no major issues even though it was an older property in the historic district, built in the 1950's. They had seven guest rooms, each with an ensuite bath, and the Boudreaux personal suite. They had a dining room, which could accommodate twenty-five. They did occasionally book wedding and baby showers, or business meetings and dinners, which helps with the income. If the Christmas-themed weekend was a hit, then other holiday stays, such as Valentine's Day, Easter, Mother's Day, Fourth of July, and others were all possibilities that the Boudreaux family hoped to market. Since their savings were almost gone, the last ditch effort was needed to work, and work well! Gustav had met with the bank in an effort to give them more time because he was trying every marketing idea he can find. To say he was nervous about this was an understatement as he truly felt it was the inn's last hope for survival.

How could it have been that difficult to make the beautiful inn profitable? It was not like they had tremendous competition in their small town. He was simply beside himself with worry, and tried to always put on a positive face for Olive, whom he loved dearly, Jackson, their only child, who helped them quite a lot, especially with social media, and their staff, whom he knew depended on their jobs for survival.

Advertising elsewhere was ridiculously expensive. They had sought out travel magazines and websites but they simply could not afford the huge cash outlays they demanded.

The holiday-themed events of that weekend took a lot of work to put together, especially the décor. But, if that weekend would prove they did appeal to travelers, then it would all be worth it.

Chapter 3:
Guest Check In

Later that afternoon, the guests begat to arrive. The first to check in was a single, middle-aged man who announced himself as Dr. Formby. He was dressed casually in jeans and a sweater. Jackson was friendly, and greeted him warmly, showing him the itinerary of all the holiday-themed events. Dr. Formby replied, "Well, I don't know about all of this as I am here for a much needed rest."

Jackson immediately replied, "But, it will be such fun starting tomorrow at the tree trimming party! Everyone will be there and it will set the tone for the festive Christmas season."

Dr. Formby reluctantly agreed to think about it. Jackson gave him his key, and pointed him in the direction of his room, the Blue Christmas Room, named, of course, for the Elvis Christmas hit. Decorated in blue and silver, it was very beautiful indeed. Dr. Formby was happy with this, and felt he could relax there, which he desperately needed. He had been so surprised upon receiving the invite for this weekend stay in the red envelope. He had checked out the Inn, and felt this just might be the Christmas miracle he needed.

Next was Lucille Chambers. With her heavy southern accent, she expressed excitement about the itinerary of events. She was dressed in a plaid flannel shirt and jeans with a cargo jacket, and asked Jackson, "Will there be time for me to forage for some mushrooms? I just adore them. Perhaps I could even supply some for a dinner."

She showed Jackson her foraging book and it was impressive. Jackson told her she would certainly have free time to do so but she would need to ask Chef Marta about including them on a menu. When Jackson gave Lucille her key, and told her she was staying in The Cardinal Room, she started crying.

Jackson immediately said, "I am so sorry! We can change you into another room. It is simply named that because of the décor."

Lucille replied, "No, I am sorry. It is just that cardinals remind me of loved ones taken from us too soon. I am certain I will love it. Thank you."

Jackson pointed her in the direction of her room, and secretly made a note to watch over Lucille Chambers. Lucille opened the door of her room, and was immediately teary eyed. Beautiful red cardinals were everywhere. She realized this trip could be a healing time for her as she had truly been lonely since her friend died, and was hopeful that this holiday would not be as sad, with new experiences and possibly making new friends. She set about unpacking, and set her letters on the night stand. She read them often to remember Alice. Then, she started checking out all the excursion ideas, and the map of the surrounding area to plan some trips. She set her foraging book on the dresser. Lucille was certain she could discover some new varieties of mushrooms there. When all was in place, she sat on the bed, and thought what a wonderful weekend this could be for her. All these holiday activities and excursions could be just what the doctor ordered. She started a gratitude list and number one on the list was the red envelope gifting her this stay.

The next guest looked somewhat familiar to Jackson and she announced herself as Raven DuPree. Raven was professionally dressed in a russet wool, plaid jacket with matching slacks, a scarf for color, classic gold jewelry, and a Louis Vuitton bag. Then, Jackson realized who she was, a famous mystery writer with many bestselling books! He welcomed her, and showed her the itinerary of events, which really seemed to interest her. He then handed her the key to The Silver Bells Room.

Raven asked Jackson to send up a printer to her room as she was behind on her writing, and would use the down times to catch up before her deadline. He promised to do so, and made himself a note. When she opened the door to a stunning room, where bells were the prevailing decorating theme, she could almost hear the song playing in her head.

She decided that would be an adequate room for her writing as she definitely would need to work, not just enjoy the planned activities. However, she planned to make notes on the holiday experiences, and how the guests related to them, as this could be valuable research for her new book. Raven knew how important it was to check into everything so she could garner as many ideas as possible. The planned holiday activities would be just the perfect research tool for her. Plus, she could enjoy them herself! She was so very thankful she noticed the pop up ads about The Mistletoe Inn. Funny how she had never seen nor heard of it before but it would be the perfect time for her to take advantage of that special weekend.

The guests kept arriving and Jackson did not have much time to think before another stepped up. This time, it is a young lady named Scarlett Johnson. Scarlett, dressed casually in leggings and a long sweater, introduced herself and Jackson found her reservation. He noticed she seemed a bit nervous, and asked if she was alright.

"Of course. Why wouldn't I be?" Scarlett responded. "It is just that this holiday can be a bit sad for those missing loved ones."

Jackson handed her the itinerary, smiled, and said, "With all of the planned events, your holiday spirit might get a real boost! Who knows? You might make a new friend or two."

Scarlett seemed much more at ease with that idea as Jackson handed her the key to the Victorian Christmas Room, and pointed her to the last room on the first floor. Scarlett opened the door, and felt like she had definitely stepped back in time. The Victorian décor was everywhere! The bed linens, the ornaments on the tree, and the colors, all harkened back to a more gentle time. Scarlett felt very cozy and at home there! She curled up on the bed, and quickly fell asleep. Her dreams were pleasant. Yes, that stay was the perfect idea for Scarlett. She would be able to enjoy all of those holiday events that she had never experienced and she would not be alone! However, while she was falling asleep, she had still been puzzling about who sent that red envelope, gifting her with this weekend. But, she was set to enjoy it!

Next in line was a well-dressed woman in designer sunglasses who introduced herself as Renata Castleberry. She was adorned with expensive jewelry, and asked about the availability of room service.

Jackson answered, "Unfortunately, no, we do not offer that service here but you are welcome to join us for all of these planned activities, which have refreshments included."

He handed Renata the itinerary and she quickly scanned it, and remarked, "Well, I see. Hmmmm, maybe this will work."

Jackson handed her the key to the Peacock Room that had all things peacock feathers, thinking how perfectly fitting this might be for her. Renata headed toward the stairs as her room was on the second floor. When Renata entered her room, she gasped as the colors were so vibrant and beautiful. The décor was something different from what she had ever experienced! From the bed to the professional decorated tree, it was both colorful and relaxing as the hues soothed her. Next, she began looking at all the activities and excursions offered to the guests. This weekend was going to be just what she needed! When the red envelope had appeared in her mailbox, she knew immediately that her husband must have arranged it so she would experience some Christmas fun even though it would be without him. Yes, Renata would be quite comfortable here even without room service. She started planning her activities, and coordinating her outfits. It was great that she brought so many because she would need them!

Nancy Ellis, the next guest, was an older woman, dressed in sweatpants and a Christmas sweatshirt, who seemed very friendly, and eager to participate in the activities on the itinerary. She asked Jackson if there was some shopping nearby because she wanted to purchase a special present for her niece. He gave her a map of the historic downtown square, and explained there were several shops there that would fit her needs, all within walking distance.

She exclaimed, "Oh, good! I will have a chance to wear my white, fur-trimmed parka that my niece gave to me." Jackson handed her the key to The Snowflake Room, and pointed her to the stairs. She walked to her room and, when she opened her door, she felt she had just entered a Winter Wonderland. It was all decorated in white, with glittery ornaments, snowflakes, and silvery strands of tinsel on the tree. She only wished her late husband was with her to enjoy the beauty. She was amazed at all the beautiful décor, and set about unpacking. His picture, her niece's picture, and the beautiful mistletoe plants were all placed atop the dresser. Next, she started planning all of her activities and shopping excursions as she read all the detailed brochures Jackson had provided to her. She would need to remember to thank her niece for this fabulous trip! It was such a surprise when the red envelope appeared. What a thoughtful gift!

The last guest approached the front desk and, before Jackson could even ask his name, he shouted, "Well, it's about time! I thought I was going to have to sleep out here. It has taken so long." Mr. Fathom was a thin, short-tempered man, dressed in rumpled clothes, who apparently did not like waiting in line to check in. Jackson apologized for the wait, handed him the itinerary, which Mr. Fathom did not even acknowledge, and the key to The Silver and Gold Room at the end of the hall, on the second floor.

As Mr. Fathom was about to take his first step up the stairs, Jackson again stopped him to give him a note that was left for him at the desk. Mr. Fathom seemed surprised, and asked who left it. Jackson replied that he did not know...perhaps a friend?

Mr. Fathom said, "I don't have any friends."

Jackson tried again, "Perhaps a family member?"

Mr. Fathom replied, "No family, either."

Jackson tried once more, "Maybe a co-worker?"

Mr. Fathom said, "No one knows I am here."

At this point, Jackson handed him the note, and said he had no idea who could have left it but it must be important, and advised Mr. Fathom to read it when he got to his room.

Mr. Fathom just grunted, and proceeded up the stairs. He knew this stay would be a mistake. The only reason he agreed to it was because his Uncle Ben, and that lawyer of his, Willingham, expected it. After the time it took for him to check in, there was no telling what other inconveniences he would face during this weekend. He would just keep a low profile, and ride this out, hoping it would not be as bad as he felt it could be. When he arrived in his room, he barely noticed the beautiful décor as he simply put his suitcase on the chair, and sat on the bed to read the note.

At this point, Jackson was quite glad there were no more guests, and remembered the printer that was requested by Raven Du Pree. He located one, delivered it to her room, and breathed a sigh of relief. This was going to be challenging with a full house of guests and all these activities. He looked at his watch. It was definitely time for a beer.

He headed to the kitchen, and helped himself, sitting down, and thinking of all the guests that were now in their rooms.

Chef Marta was already gone for the evening so he had the kitchen to himself. He was still thinking when Gustav came in. "How did check in go?" he asked.

Jackson replied, "Challenging to say the least."

Gustav poured himself a glass of wine, and pulled up a chair. "In what way?"

Jackson told him about each guest, their demeanor, how they reacted to the scheduled events. When he got to Mr. Fathom, he told Gustav, "Good luck making him happy! He is an odd duck if you ask me."

Gustav wanted to know why Jackson thought so poorly of Mr. Fathom. Jackson filled him in on his grumpy behavior, and him seemingly not having any family or friends, etc. He finished by saying, "I just have a bad feeling about him. I know that these reviews are crucial to our financial situation so I know that we need to do everything to make sure the guests are happy, but, with that one, I am not so sure we are capable of making him happy."

Gustav listened, and said he and Olive would try to make sure to include Mr. Fathom in everything, hoping he would make a friend, or at least an acquaintance.

Chapter 4:
Jeff Willingham, J.D.

Jeff Willingham was a well-respected lawyer in Oklahoma whose clients included wealthy business owners like Ben Cooper, the uncle of Mr. Fathom who was staying at The Mistletoe Inn. Mr. Cooper had recently sold his large paper plate production plant to an industry giant for a multimillion dollar sum, adding to his already substantial wealth. Jeff worked out all the details of this sale from start to finish, earning a hefty profit himself. He then was charged with another special project from Mr. Cooper who has recently been placed on hospice care as his health has been declining for some time. The special project was to coordinate a surprise meeting of five individuals with Mr. Fathom, hopefully to heal some old wounds, and allow for closure and new beginnings for all of them.

Ben Cooper was well respected in the community but, in his early years, he was known to be quite ruthless with the people surrounding him. He never married, or had any children, hence his concern for his nephew. He was known to be a cruel task master to his employees and to anyone he did business with. However, one Christmas his heart was totally changed. After that, Ben was truly a new man, generous to all of his employees, their families, and to the community.

Jeff had, over the years, kept Ben abreast of Mr. Fathom's affairs and this led to Ben's concern for his nephew making the same mistakes that he had, and possibly even worse. This saddened Ben as he thought of all the years wasted being alone. So, he'd planned this "surprise" to hopefully change his nephew's heart. Jeff warned Ben of the potential danger of bringing all those people together under a false pretense and the explosive emotion that could emerge from such a meeting as this. But, Ben was positive that such a ruse was completely necessary to get everyone together at one place and at one time during the holiday season. He felt it the best chance to redeem his nephew before it was too late.

The plan was simple, really. Ben had Jeff send out five gift certificates, one for each of the people his nephew had wronged, for a holiday-themed stay at The Mistletoe Inn. They were not to know who had sent them, each guessing someone else and, hopefully, they would seek out this holiday-themed weekend as being just what they needed for a break from their troubled lives.

The sixth individual lured there was a famed mystery writer who Jeff inundated with pop up ads for The Mistletoe Inn in the hopes that she would deem it a perfect research trip. That way, all of it could be documented, and would possibly make a great inspirational book or movie to inspire others.

Jeff sent the payments to The Mistletoe Inn from a private company called Blue Skies Investments, LLC to keep anyone from finding out why they were selected, and by whom. Jeff was worried about the outcome of this risky surprise meeting, but was followed out his client's wishes to the letter.

Unfortunately, the day before the guests were to arrive, Ben Cooper sadly passed away. Jeff was notified immediately, and sent word to Mr. Fathom in the form of a note that his uncle had passed Unfortunately, since the stipulation of inheriting was for Fathom to have made things right with the five people, what would happen to his uncle's fortune?

Chapter 5:
Lucille Chambers

Lucille Chambers had recently moved to Wimberley, in the Texas Hill Country, after retiring. She loved her life there, especially her hobby, which was foraging for mushrooms. But, she still kept in touch with some of her friends, one of whom recently had taken her own life after a terrible ordeal at work. Lucille was still in shock over this loss as her friend did not exhibit the worrying behavior of someone contemplating suicide.

Lucille was determined in the new year to investigate the circumstances, and see if she could possibly start to understand what had happened. She knew her friend worked for a terrible boss who was demanding, and would not have been empathetic to a depressed employee. Her friend had confided in her many times of her frustrations of working there. Lucille had tried to talk her into finding another job and she had promised to look into it in the new year. Then, sadly, she had taken her own life, leaving no note of explanation other than a journal of sad thoughts. Lucille treasured her friend's memory, and kept her letters, searching them for clues of her mental breakdown.

Lucille was hoping to enjoy this holiday season even with the sad loss of her friend by coming on this holiday-themed weekend. All those activities might help her feel more festive; at least that was her hope. What was strange was the timing of the invitation and who could have sent it?

Chapter 6:
The Tree Trimming Party

On Thursday afternoon, the inn was busy with preparations for the first event of the Christmas-themed stay: The Tree Trimming Party.

A large Christmas tree was securely positioned in the lobby, the Chef was busy making Christmas cookies, and the smells that kept drifting out of the kitchen were unmistakable. Bambi Lynn was making sure everything was perfectly positioned, that the decorations were all laid out, and that the popcorn bowl and the cranberries were all there just waiting to be strung. Jackson was ready to start the Christmas music playing with his play list all queued up.

Just before 7:00, the guests began arriving, having had a fun day of exploring on their own. By 7:15, all but two guests were present, ready to decorate. Jackson noticed that both Dr. Formby and Mr. Fathom were missing, and decided to go and remind them both. Knocking on Dr. Formby's door, Jackson called out, "Dr. Formby, it is Jackson here to remind you of the tree trimming party. Everyone is downstairs decorating, enjoying Christmas cookies, and spiked cider. You do not want to miss this."

Dr. Formby opened his door, and replied, "Well, I do like cookies. I guess it wouldn't hurt to join in for a bit." Dr. Formby then proceeded to join the others in the tree decorating. Guests were stringing popcorn and cranberries to make festive garlands, hanging ornaments, and, of course, enjoying the cookies and cider that Chef Marta prepared. Dr. Formby found he was enjoying himself more than he had in a very long time.

Next, Jackson went upstairs to Mr. Fathom's room. He knocked, and called out to Mr. Fathom the same as he had with Dr. Formby. No reply. He knocked again and called out to Mr. Fathom. Again, no reply. He did notice a silver tray sitting outside the doorway, and thought that a bit odd since The Mistletoe Inn did not offer room service. But, after the way Mr. Fathom had acted at check in, he just assumed that he had demanded the chef send him some food as he certainly did not want to join the others. Jackson gave up, and went back downstairs to join everyone else.

When he arrived downstairs, he pulled Gustav aside to tell him that Mr. Fathom did not answer and that he had a funny feeling about him, reminding him of the way he'd acted at check-in the previous day. Gustav told him maybe he just wanted to be left alone, not to worry, and to just enjoy the party with the other guests. So, Jackson put his worries aside, and joined in the merriment with the six guests and the staff.

The highlight was the famed local entertainer, Charlotte Champion, singing for everyone. She was definitely a hit with the guests and everyone had a great time, staying until after 9:00. There was no sign of Mr. Fathom during the party at all. Everyone was enjoying themselves so much that no one noticed when one of the guests silently snuck away for a few minutes.

Gustav, Olive, Bambi Lynn, and Jackson all stayed late to clean up, remarking what a wonderful event it was and how much the guests seemed to enjoy it. They talked about ways of making it even better for the next group of guests. Then, they also talked about the next event, the scavenger hunt, and how it was shaping up. Jackson was busy with printing the clues that Gustav had arranged, and assembling the prize bag for the winner. So many of the downtown shops had contributed to the prize that it really was grand.

Chef Marta had earlier assured them that she would have hot chocolate and smores around the fire pit waiting for the guests after their successful return. Olive was in charge of transporting the guests to the historic downtown square where the scavenger hunt would take place. Everyone understood the plan, and finally went home (the Boudreauxs to their quarters), confident about the next day.

Chapter 7:
The Next Day

The following morning's breakfast was served to 6 and, of the guests, Mr. Fathom was again absent. As breakfast service was winding down, Dr. Formby was headed to his room when, all of the sudden, he heard a scream coming from upstairs. Being a doctor, he rushed up the stairs to find Bambi Lynn crying, and pointing to Mr. Fathom, who looked to be dead in his bed. His eyes were wide open, as was his mouth, seemingly in horror. His lifeless body was in his bed, garishly posed like in a movie. What had happened? What had frightened him so?

Dr. Formby went to check his pulse, and determined that he, indeed, was dead and, since Gustav had joined them after hearing the scream as well, he asked Gustav to call for an ambulance, stating that they had an unresponsive guest.

When Gustav phoned, the 911 operator asked if he was sure that Mr. Fathom was, in fact, dead. He said yes and that there was a doctor who pronounced him dead on the premises. Then, she said she would have the ambulance get there as quickly as possible.

By now, all the guests had gathered outside the room to see what the scream and fuss was about. Bambi Lynn was still quite upset and Olive was trying to comfort her. Dr. Formby was trying to keep the guests out of the room, explaining that they were waiting for the ambulance. Raven DuPree waltzed right into the room anyway, offering her help to everyone in case this was a crime scene as she was known to have helped police solve crimes before. They assured her this was not known to be a crime scene, and to wait outside with everyone else.

Soon, the EMTs charged up the stairs, and checked on the body to confirm he was deceased. Then, they called the detective to join them, as well as sent all the guests to their rooms, except for Dr. Formby as he was the first to examine the body after Bambi Lynn screamed.

Detective Chestnut, a seasoned member of the Jeffersonville P.D., arrived on the scene moments later with her assistant, Gary. She immediately checked the body herself, and spoke to Bambi Lynn, who told her that she just knocked on Mr. Fathom's door to announce she would be cleaning his room. When there was no answer, she used her key to unlock the room, and found him lying there. That is when she screamed.

Detective Chestnut asked her if she touched anything. She answered, "NO! I just screamed when I saw him lying there like he was dead!"

Then, Dr. Formby told the detective he was quickly on the scene after the scream and, other than checking Mr. Fathom's pulse, did not touch anything himself.

Looking around the room, the detective saw a tray with a plate, and an empty glass on the night stand. After putting on gloves, she picked up the glass, sniffed it, and asked her assistant, Gary, to bag both for prints. She then asked, "Who is the owner of The Mistletoe Inn?"

Gustav and Olive stepped forward to tell her how long they had owned it. She asked them, "Who delivered this tray?"

They both looked at Chef Marta, who answered, "Me. I delivered it yesterday to him. He called down, and requested it. I told him we do not normally provide an evening meal, just breakfast, but he insisted he was starving. So, since I was already in the kitchen working on the snacks for the tree trimming party, I told him I would make him a turkey sandwich. He also requested a soda. I said I could do that, and delivered it to his door."

Detective Chestnut asked, "What time was that?"

Chef Marta answered quickly, "It was at 6:30. I remember because I had to have all of the cookies and cider ready by 6:45."

Detective Chestnut asked, "How did he seem when he received the food?"

Chef Marta replied, "That was the odd thing. I knocked loudly, and called him to the door but he did not answer so I left it in the doorway."

"You just left it in the doorway?" asked Detective Chestnut.

"Yes, but it was covered and everyone was on their way down to the party anyway so I thought there would be no harm," answered Chef Marta.

Detective Chestnut continued, "You do realize that any other guest or staff member would have had access to this food and drink?"

"Surely you do not think that any of our guests or staff would contaminate his food," said Gustav, incredulously.

Detective Chestnut replied, "I have no idea. I am just stating the obvious danger of leaving a tray out in the open with anyone having access to it. We will know more when the coroner examines the body. I need to speak to everyone who had any contact with Mr. Fathom, starting with the front desk person."

Jackson stepped up, and introduced himself to her. He then told her the odd behavior of Mr. Fathom at check in and how he did not respond to the tree trimming party invitation, nor to the knock on his door during the party to check on him.

Gustav then intervened, saying that he had assumed Mr. Fathom did not want to be disturbed, and asked Jackson not to bother him again.

Jackson then told Detective Chestnut about the note left for Mr. Fathom at check in. "What did the note say?" asked the detective.

"I have no idea as I did not read it before I handed it to him. All I know is his reaction was so incredibly strange, saying he basically had no one."

"Where is this note now?" asked Detective Chestnut. Gary looked under Mr. Fathom's bed, and found a crumpled note. He handed it to Detective Chestnut.

After reading it, she exclaimed, "Well, he certainly *did* have someone, but not now. He only had a fortune since his uncle died yesterday, and left all his money to him."

This certainly changed the tone in the room because everyone then knew they might be dealing with a crime scene. Detective Chestnut had Gary bag the note for prints, and told the EMT to please remove Mr. Fathom's body, and take him straight to the coroner's office. The EMT brought in the stretcher, and removed Mr. Fathom's body. Detective Chestnut then told Gustav that this room was considered a crime scene and that she wanted the room dusted for prints, and searched from top to bottom. Gary began his search as she then asked Gustav to let her speak to each guest separately.

Chapter 8:
Dr. Formby

Dr. Formby was a general practitioner whose practice was in a small town in East Texas. He had built his practice after taking over from a retired, beloved physician ten years prior. Dr. Formby had become accepted by the residents, and had many satisfied patients of all ages. He was single and, as such, lots of the older patients would bring him casseroles and desserts regularly. He loved that attention.

However, two years previously, a young woman came to see him because she had suddenly developed some disturbing troubles swallowing and she was hiccupping uncontrollably. Dr. Formby was convinced that she suffered from acid reflux, and prescribed some medications that should have worked well for her. But, before her next scheduled appointment, she called to say she was worse. When she told him her symptoms, Dr. Formby advised her to go to the ER. She did and they ran several tests, concluding she had esophageal cancer. Her family was devastated and, six months later, she passed away.

Dr. Formby took the news very hard indeed, and would constantly go over and over her symptoms again, trying to see if he missed something obvious. To make matters worse, two months prior, he received a notice that he was being placed on suspension due to a malpractice claim regarding her death.

So, for the past two months, Dr. Formby had been a recluse. Feeling so bad for the woman's family and fiancée (later he learned she had just gotten engaged), he just kept to himself. He used delivery services for everything, not wanting to show his face in public in that small town. When he received the invitation to an inn miles away, he felt like it was the best gift anyone had ever given him, a respite from all the small town gossip and heartache. He certainly needed some holiday spirit so he was happy to take advantage of such a gift, anonymous as it was.

At the inn, no one would know him, or about his current situation, and he could just rest, relax, and enjoy this holiday weekend without fear of gossip and innuendos. But, when he heard the dead man's name, he recognized it immediately. It was true that he had never met Mr. Fathom, but certainly knew he was the person who filed the malpractice claim. Apparently, it was his fiancée who passed from cancer. Now, he was the one pronouncing Mr. Fathom dead. This made Dr. Formby quite nervous indeed. He was certain that any investigation would uncover the malpractice claim, and his ties to the deceased.

Chapter 9:
The Investigation

Gustav offered to go with Detective Chestnut but she instead had him bring her the check-in register and payment logs. She also asked for a chair and a small table in the hallway on each floor so she could interview the guests. Jackson went to work making those available while Gustav hurried off to the lobby and office to find the register and logs. Detective Chestnut waited in the hall until she had the items, and began to find each guest.

Detective Chestnut knocked on Room 1. Dr. Formby answered. She asked him to join her in the hall, sitting in the chair. "Dr. Formby, what brings you to The Mistletoe Inn?" she asked.

He replied, "I received this stay from one of my patients who knew I needed a break. It was a lovely Christmas gift."

"What was the patient's name?" she asked.

He replied, "It was anonymous so I have no idea."

Detective Chestnut continued, "You are an MD?"

"Yes, a General Practitioner," replied Dr. Formby.

"Do your patients give you gifts like this often?" the detective asked.

"No, certainly not. But, as I stated, I have been overworked, and needed a break. Perhaps the patient was sensitive to my situation."

"Were you familiar with Mr. Fathom?" asked Detective Chestnut.

"No, not at all," said Dr. Formby.

"You have never met him before?" continued Detective Chestnut.

"No, I saw him at breakfast yesterday, sitting by himself, and that was the only time I had ever seen him until today when I heard the scream, and came running to see what had happened, and if I could help in any way. I could clearly see his state, and checked his pulse to be sure before pronouncing him dead," answered Dr. Formby.

"One more question," said Detective Chestnut. "Did you see or hear anything out of the ordinary last night?"

Dr. Formby thought for a moment, and said, "No. I came in from the tree trimming party, and went almost immediately to bed after the cookies and spiked cider. I slept like a baby."

Detective Chestnut was satisfied with his answers so she thanked him for his help, and went to the next room. She knocked on the door and asked Lucille Chambers to come out into the hallway, and sit down to interview her. Detective Chestnut started out asking who she was.

"I am Lucille Chambers from Wimberley, here for the holiday themed weekend," she stated.

The detective answered, "From Wimberley. Hmm... How did you find out about The Mistletoe Inn?"

Lucille continued, "That was the strangest thing. I received this beautiful invitation to join in this special weekend and someone gifted it to me; not sure who."

Detective Chestnut asked, "Do you, by any chance, have that beautiful invitation with you?"

"Why, yes, I do. I brought it just in case it was a prank or something" Lucille answered. She then reached into her purse,

Mistletoe, Murder, and Mayhem

and produced a card inviting her to this holiday themed weekend stay.

"May I keep this?" asked the detective.

"Most certainly," said Lucille.

"Did you know the deceased Mr. Fathom?" asked the detective.

"No. I just saw him sitting alone at breakfast yesterday. I felt sorry for him as the rest of us joined the tree trimming party, and had a great time. Not him. He did not come at all."

"Anything else you remember about Mr. Fathom?" asked the detective.

"No. He was just alone. That is all," answered Lucille.

"Did you hear or see anything last night, anything odd?" asked Detective Chestnut.

Lucille spoke, "Not at all. I came in from the tree trimming party full of cookies and cider, and went right to bed. I slept through the night, and did not awaken until this morning."

The detective thanked her, and moved on to the next person, a name she recognized, Raven DuPree. She knocked on the door and Raven answered. She asked her to step out into the hall, and take a seat. Raven complied, but brought a notebook with her.

Detective Chestnut asked for her name and what had brought her to The Mistletoe Inn.

"Raven DuPree and I am here doing research for my next novel," she replied.

Detective Chestnut continued, "Did you receive an invitation to come here this weekend?"

"No, should I have?" Raven replied, and continued, "I saw some pop up ads about this particular weekend and, since my next novel is a Christmas themed mystery, I thought it seemed the perfect setting for my research."

Detective Chestnut continued, "Did you know the deceased Mr. Fathom?"

Raven replied, "No, I have never seen him before. He ate breakfast yesterday alone, not speaking with anyone so no one could have gotten to know him. I assumed he was a recluse, and wanted to be left alone so I never even approached him."

The detective asked another question, "Did you happen to see or hear anything strange last night?"

Raven answered, "Well, I was up late writing because I have a looming deadline for my next book, and thought I heard a door slam, and some coughing very late. But, it went away after just a couple of minutes so I assumed someone had allergies."

Detective Chestnut asked, "What time was that?"

Raven answered, "Not totally sure, but probably about 1:00." Detective Chestnut thanked her, and was about to go to the next person when Raven asked, "Do you need some investigating help? I have been very effective with other agencies investigating murders, and would be more than happy to be of service to you."

Detective Chestnut rolled her eyes, and said, "That will not be necessary. No one has said anything about murder and I will handle any investigating that needs to happen. That will be all."

Raven rolled her eyes in return, and went back into her room.

Chapter 10:
Raven DuPree

Raven DuPree, the famous mystery writer, was a high school English teacher for 20 years. She had always dreamed of writing a novel, and then, one day, she did! She navigated her way through the publishing world, and was picked up by a New York firm that immediately saw her talent. She became a New York Times bestselling author of eleven books, and was also known for assisting the police in solving some murder cases. Raven made friends with a NYPD detective who used her to consult, and find clues the department may have missed, overlooked, or deemed unimportant.

Raven was researching a Christmas murder mystery because those were very popular. She felt the time was right for her to delve into this specialized mystery genre. One day, as she was researching locations, some ads popped up on her computer advertising The Mistletoe Inn, with its Christmas themed long weekend stays. The activities advertised seemed perfect for getting into the Christmas spirit and she thought it might give her some good ideas for her story. Being from the East Coast, Raven also felt this might be a great new adventure; Christmas in Texas.

She was well respected in New York circles but, in small town Texas, not so much. Detective Chestnut made this quite clear. Still, she was willing to give it one more try as she felt compelled to help since she was a guest at the same bed and breakfast.

Raven was a widow with no children. Her husband had died of a heart attack many years ago at home and, shortly afterward, Raven learned CPR. She wanted to help, if needed, to save someone's life since she never got the chance to save her husband.

Maybe if she shared her personal story with Detective Chestnut the following day, she would be open to her helping in this case rather than the detective assuming Raven wanted to take over. Also, she would personally guarantee not to use any of this story in her book, which might have been a concern as well. If need be, she would ask her NYPD friend to talk on her behalf as well to allay any fears Detective Chestnut might have in trusting her instincts.

Raven spent quite a while mulling over each guest at The Mistletoe Inn, and thinking of what their motive could possibly be to kill that difficult man, Mr. Fathom. She also researched him on her laptop thoroughly and was surprised at what she found. Yes, she could definitely help Detective Chestnut if she would let her, especially now that she had information to share. She made a plan to ask Gustav to drive her to police headquarters the following day, immediately after breakfast

The next room was Scarlett Johnson's. Detective Chestnut knocked, and requested Ms. Johnson join her in the hallway. She sat down and Detective Chestnut began, "Ms. Johnson, what brought you to The Mistletoe Inn?"

Scarlett answered, "It is Miss Johnson and I received a sweet gift certificate in the mail to enjoy this holiday weekend. I have no idea who sent it."

Detective Chestnut answered, "May I see the gift certificate please?"

"Why yes, Detective. I have it with me to show to the front desk. Here it is." Scarlett handed Detective Chestnut the same invitation she has seen before.

"Just as I thought," said the detective. "I have seen this before. Are you certain you do not know who sent it?"

"Well, of course not! Why? What do you mean you have seen this before?" Scarlett acted very surprised to hear that.

Detective Chestnut replied, "I will ask the questions here. Did you know the deceased Mr. Fathom?"

Scarlett answered, "No, not at all, I only saw him yesterday at breakfast, just sitting alone. He did not join in the tree trimming party with everyone else. We had such a good time."

Detective Chestnut continued, "Did you hear or see anything unusual last night?"

Scarlett answered, "Well, now that you mention it, I did hear a door slam very late but that was all."

Detective Chestnut asked her, "What time did you hear that?"

Scarlett thought for a moment and answered, "I'm not sure but maybe 1:00 or so as I was just barely asleep. I read for a while before falling asleep and it was late when I did go to sleep."

The detective thanked Scarlett, and went up the stairs to the next guest, Renata Castleberry. She knocked on the door, and asked Ms. Castleberry to come out, and sit in a chair in the hallway. "Ms. Castleberry, tell me what brought you to The Mistletoe Inn."

Renata answered, "Well, that is a great story. I received a very generous gift certificate for this holiday weekend stay anonymously, although I am quite sure it is something my late husband had planned for me. He was very generous indeed, and would want me to carry on enjoying myself, especially knowing how much I loved Christmas."

Detective Chestnut asked to see the gift certificate and Renata went into her room to retrieve it. "I brought it with me just in case there was any question," she offered as she handed it to the detective.

Detective Chestnut took a look, recognizing it immediately as the exact same as the others. She asked, "Are you certain this is from your husband?"

Renata bristled at the idea that it would be from anyone else. She replied, "Of COURSE I am certain. He always wanted me to have the very best of everything so why wouldn't he provide one last surprise for me?"

Detective Chestnut went to the next question. "Did you happen to know the deceased Mr. Fathom?"

Renata answered, "No, I had never seen him before breakfast yesterday when he insisted on sitting alone, not even making eye contact with anyone. Who would want to even try to get to know someone like that?"

Detective Chestnut continued, "Did you see or hear anything unusual last night?"

Renata answered, "Do you mean the door slamming, and the gasping and coughing at 1:00 in the morning? Yes, I certainly did. It woke me up. But, by the time I put my robe on, and opened my door, there was no sound at all and no one in the hallway. I guessed everything was then okay so I returned to my bed, and slept the rest of the night."

Detective Chestnut thanked her, and went to the next room, a Nancy Ellis. She knocked, and asked Ms. Ellis to join her in the hallway. When she was sitting in the chair, Detective Chestnut began, "Ms. Ellis, please tell me what brought you to The Mistletoe Inn."

Nancy answered, "My wonderful niece gifted me this stay as she knew I was all alone and she spoils me so, especially during the holidays."

Detective Chestnut continued, "Did she send you an invite to this particular weekend?"

Nancy answered, "Why, yes. Here it is in my purse. I brought it just in case I needed to give it to the front desk at check in."

The detective looked, again seeing the exact same invite as the others. "Are you sure this was from your niece?"

Nancy answered, "Well, of course she denied it, but she loves to surprise me, so it must be from her."

Detective Chestnut continued, "Did you know the deceased Mr. Fathom?"

Nancy replied, "No, but I certainly tried. I went over to his table at breakfast yesterday, and tried to join him. He would not even look at me. I just assumed he was a loner, and wanted to be left in peace so I joined another table. These guests, aside from him, are all lovely. I am truly enjoying myself. The tree trimming party was so much fun. I can hardly wait until today's scavenger hunt! More fun for sure."

Detective Chestnut asked Nancy if she had heard anything the previous night.

Nancy replied, "Well, I am quite a sound sleeper but I did hear something odd, like coughing or gasping, sounding like it was coming from his room. But, it stopped after a few seconds and then all was quiet so I thought maybe I dreamed it. Why, is that how he passed?"

Detective Chestnut answered, "We are not sure of anything right now. I'm just trying to piece together the night before he was found deceased. Thank you, that will be all for now."

Chapter 11:
Mr. Fathom

Nigel Fathom was a middle-aged man who was definitely a loner. He never married, nor had any children, and was generally not very pleasant to anyone. Nigel was engaged once. However, his fiancé died of an undetected cancer. From that day forward, he was alone. He was a shrewd businessman who was known to demand the best of everyone who worked for him, and any vendor that supplied his company.

Nigel owned a pharmaceutical company that was trying to be on the cutting edge of many things. A cure for this or that could definitely put him on top of his competition if (and this was a big if) he was the first to discover and market it. Pharmaceutical companies are very competitive, always trying to be the first to develop and market something new that the public needed. But, along with the research and technology come physical trials and FDA approvals, which can take years to complete. Cutting corners with the trials, or manipulating the records could be very dangerous as drugs could prove to be more harmful than good.

Nigel Fathom was not a patient man and his employees all knew it. He demanded the new potential drugs be in trials sometimes before they were ready, according to his researchers, who urged him to wait a bit longer for more data. The trials often took place in third-world countries where many volunteer for trials to earn any extra money for their families. Occasionally, he would have an employee volunteer if the drug was not considered life threatening, which was the case with the male pattern baldness drug that his company had tried the previous year. Unfortunately, one of his employees had a terrible reaction to the drug, and died.

Nigel's only living relative was an uncle, Ben Cooper, who was quite wealthy. Mr. Cooper made his living in paper products and he always was concerned about his nephew being alone. He would contact him from time to time, and arrange a meeting to check on him, especially after the death of Nigel's fiancée. Mr. Cooper had asked his longtime lawyer and personal friend, Jeff Willingham, to start checking on his nephew, which was how he uncovered several instances of unresolved conflicts. Mr. Cooper and Jeff devised a plan to help his nephew reconcile with those people and, thus, turn over a new leaf, which was his uncle's most urgent wish as he seriously wanted his nephew to be happy.

Unfortunately, now that Nigel Fathom was dead, those matters would remain unresolved.

Chapter 12:
More Questions

When Detective Chestnut finished interviewing the guests, she went back downstairs to locate the owners. Gustav and Olive were waiting to speak with her and they were anxious to hear what she thought of the guests. They were anxious and nervous, especially Olive. No inn owner would want a murder taking place on their property, especially ones that were close to bankruptcy. Also, no one wanted to think that they were in the same building as a murderer.

Gustav asked, "Well, did you learn anything from our guests?"

Detective Chestnut answered, "I am not sure yet...early on in the investigation. But, a curious thing has popped up. Are you aware that several of the guests who were invited here received the same invitation? Here is one for you to see. Apparently, the same person must have paid for these rooms. Can you check and see?"

Gustav was taken aback by this news. He and Olive immediately took the detective to the office, and pulled up the bank records. "Yes, I see that now. A company by the name Blue Skies Investments paid for six rooms online and Raven Du Pree paid for hers separately," said Olive.

"What do you know about Blue Skies Investments? Who are they? Have they booked rooms before?" Detective Chestnut asked.

Olive looked back at their files, and answered, "No record of them before. I have never heard of them. Must not be local."

Detective Chestnut answered, "Hmmmm... Very interesting. Also, it seems that the note to the deceased was from a similar hand. Connection? Not sure, but worth checking out. None of the guests claim to know the deceased. Will know more when the coroner finishes the examination. I will head to my office now, and await the findings from the coroner. I will be in touch with you should I need to come back, and ask more questions."

Detective Chestnut left and Olive was a basket case. "Now what are we going to do? We need to investigate ourselves, too! We could have a mass murderer on our property!" She started weeping. Gustav held her for a minute, and then told her to pull herself together. They still had six guests to take care of, and a planned scavenger hunt for that evening.

Olive reluctantly agreed, and went to finish the details for that night. She needed to get the scavenger hunt clues from Jackson, and check with Chef Marta to make sure the smores ingredients and hot chocolate would be waiting upon their return.

Gustav was hoping and praying that Mr. Fathom would be found to have died of natural causes and all this talk of murder would stop before things got any worse. He did not know how much bad press The Mistletoe Inn could take before they were forced into bankruptcy.

Was Olive right? Should they suspect one of the guests of murder? It seems incredulous to him but, stranger things have happened. After all, did they *really* know anything about these guests? Of course not. He decided not to tell Olive any of this. It would just make things worse as she was already nervous, and jumping to conclusions. No one had said Mr. Fathom was murdered. For all they know, he simply passed in his sleep. Now, Chef Marta leaving that tray out in the hallway... That was a bad business but surely that was not the cause...or was it? Gustav vowed to have a serious talk with her so she would never do that again.

Later that afternoon, Jackson got a call at the front desk. It was Detective Chestnut, asking for Gustav. Jackson called him to the phone, and heard him say, "Oh, of course, Detective. We have our guests going on a scavenger hunt starting at 4 p.m. Be here at 4:15 p.m.? They will be gone until 7:00 to 7:30 p.m. Surely that will be enough time. Okay, see you then." Gustav hung up the phone, and went to find Olive.

Gustav found Olive in the office, closed the door, and told her that the detective was coming back with a search warrant for the entire premises. It seemed Mr. Fathom was poisoned but they did not yet know exactly the type of poison that was used. They were still waiting on more tests. Olive was beside herself, and started wringing her hands. Gustav took her into his arms, and promised to handle things with the detective if she could chaperone the guests downtown for the scavenger hunt.

Olive agreed reluctantly, saying that maybe this would take their mind off of dead bodies. The plan was set. She was to transport the guests in their van at 4:00, the detective would arrive at 4:15, and leave before 7:00. She was not to mention this to any of the guests or staff so as not to alarm anyone. She nodded, realizing the serious implications of this search. What would the detective find, she wondered? Well, at least they would not have to wait much longer to find out. Maybe it would all be settled that evening! She would hold on to that ray of hope, but also decided that she would help investigate any way that she could. After all, she watched murder mysteries on TV all the time. What is the first thing they do in an investigation? Build a murder board. That was correct. She would start one herself, and try to keep an eye on all six of the guests who were now potential suspects.

Olive found a rolling dry erase board, and proceeded to build a murder board. Amazingly, it kept her busy until it was almost time to leave. She would show Gustav upon their return that night.

Chapter 13:
Scarlett Johnson

Scarlett was the youngest of the guests at The Mistletoe Inn. She was alone, with no significant other, and no family. When she received the mysterious invite, she was nervous, but also hopeful that she then had some holiday plans that might lead to making a new friend.

Scarlett's parents were killed in an auto accident many years prior and, since she was an only child, her holidays were mainly just days spent at home with a book, or watching a movie. Her parents left her well taken care of financially so Scarlett completed her education at a well-known private school, and lived in the same house she grew up in.

She kept to herself. Her favorite hobby was using essential oils, and blending them to make new natural healing formulas. She sold her blends at the local farmer's market, and felt like she was helping others with healing from nature, rather than pharmaceuticals. This gave her life purpose and she was kept busy so that she did not feel so alone. When she saw that awful man in the dining room that first breakfast, she could not help but stare at him, hoping to make eye contact. He was a loner, but seemed very practiced at it. If his name had not been visible, she would not have known he was the owner of Live Well Pharmaceuticals, whom she had researched extensively. They were known for rushing drugs to market, no matter the consequences. Maybe if she could have spoken to him, she could have helped him at least see there were alternatives that could actually help people. But, now he was dead.

Chapter 14:
Chef Marta

Chef Marta was feeling very nervous indeed after this morning's findings and the detective making her look bad for leaving the tray in the doorway. What was she supposed to do? The guest was insistent on the food, she knocked more than twice, and he did not answer. She had things to do. She could not just stand out in the hallway all night. The food was covered anyway.

But, now, Gustav was upset, and berated her as well. She apologized profusely, and promised it would never happen again. He did not say why he was so upset. Surely, he did not think the food was tainted in any way. Regardless, she was indeed nervous as she was getting things ready for the smores and hot chocolate for that night.

Marta Alvarez was also nervous for another reason. She *really* needed that job for many reasons, not the least of which was her family. She was the breadwinner at home and her elderly mom, and her two teenagers, depended on her income. Her husband was deported to Mexico, leaving her, her mom, and the children. Marta was a U.S. citizen, but *another* reason she was nervous was because she was a felon.

Marta had been a chef for a long time at a senior living facility and everything was fine...until it wasn't. Marta had been accused of harboring a fugitive. Her husband was found to be in the U.S. illegally when he was accused of stealing jewelry and other valuables from one of the residents. Marta's husband was the head of maintenance at the same facility, and was found in possession of a ruby necklace, which one of the residents claimed had been stolen. Rather than face the accusations with a detective, he ran to a private location and Marta alone knew where he was. She, of course, lied to the detective time and again and that went on for months. Eventually, they found him, checked his papers, immediately deported him, and charged Marta as his accomplice, and with harboring a fugitive, which was a felony. Marta was still on probation, and could not afford to have another charge or she would be returned to jail and her family would suffer.

When Marta applied for The Mistletoe Inn chef job, she did not exactly tell them the truth. She told them that her husband was dead and that she was a single parent with an elderly mother to take care of. She cooked a breakfast for Gustav and Olive that was delicious and they hired her immediately, without checking her references, except for personal ones. She had mentioned that she was let go from her previous job when new ownership came in and that there was no one left that she had worked with. In that, she was correct. After the stolen jewelry scandal, a new owner took over, cleaned house of all the staff, and hired new people.

Marta loved working for Gustav and Olive, especially getting to plan these special holiday activities like the ones that weekend. She was praying the job would last forever, or at least for the foreseeable future. Could this one incident prove to be the end of this wonderful job? She was hoping and praying not. Maybe if she really made the next two events extra special, the focus would not be on the leaving out of the tray. What would the detective find out about her? Hopefully, she would focus on all of the guests, and not the staff. After all, they had never heard of the deceased Mr. Fathom before. Why would any of them have a reason to kill him?

Chapter 15:
The Scavenger Hunt

At 4:00 p.m., the six guests all gathered in the lobby where Gustav, Olive, and Jackson were waiting. Gustav explained the rules to them, Jackson handed out the clues, and Olive led them to the van to transport them downtown to the historic square. The guests all seemed excited, even Dr. Formby, who, by now, seemed to be having a great time with the others. Everyone was studying their clues, and planning their first moves. When they arrived downtown, Olive told them where to meet back when they were finished, then proceeded to get herself a warm drink from the coffee shop for her wait. She planned to use her time wisely, thinking of each guest, and possible motives and opportunities for them to have poisoned Mr. Fathom. She proceeded to make notes on each guest from what she had observed. She would transfer them to her murder board when she returned home.

Dr. Formby started out at the old historic court house, finding two of the clues there, and then headed to a specialty store for another clue. He found himself immersed in the ambience of those places, and ceased worrying about the investigation.

Lucille started out at an antique store, finding an interesting clue, and enjoying conversation with the owners. She then proceeded to the local butcher shop where another clue was found. This was fun! She had not been on a scavenger hunt since she was a teenager. Also on the lookout for gifts for friends and neighbors, she was very happy indeed with her unique finds.

Scarlett began at the site of a historic prison, and became interested in the stories of all the famous people who had been kept in those walls. She then made her way to the old courthouse to find two more clues. She was becoming quite the sleuth! She then moved on to a specialty store with an antique bank vault for clue number four. After that, she treated herself to some refreshments, and continued her search for the clues.

Raven DuPree was interested in the downtown historic square for many reasons. Finding clues in the shops was simply the icing on the cake. She was making notes about all of her conversations. Apparently, some of the shops and locations were thought to be haunted. That definitely interested her and she was checking those locations out thoroughly.

Renata was enjoying all the beautiful boutiques and jewelry stores around the square. She treated herself to a fancy cocktail at a speakeasy, and found a clue there as well. While listening as someone entered, she overheard the secret password, and easily gained entrance. How exciting! She could live somewhere like that town, and start over. No one would know her past. She spent her time imagining her new life, and found a few clues. She enjoyed the time immensely!

Nancy Ellis wanted more than anything to find her niece the perfect present. So, as she was searching for clues, she, too, was shopping. She loved the boutiques and specialty stores that the historic square had to offer. From antiques, to modern day books, to art of all kinds, those places had so much to offer. As she found the clue for the old bank vault, she found that store a treasure trove of unique finds, decided on something very special for her niece, and then found the best coffee spot ever, surrounded by live plants. She paused there to enjoy the ambience, and think of all she had seen. She simply would have to bring her niece to this magical place that offered so much to see and do.

Sheila Williamson

At almost 7:00, all six made their way to find Olive. They were all happy, most of them carrying packages, and chatting away while they loaded up in the van. It seemed Scarlett had found all the clues, and in record time. So, she was declared the winner and they headed back to The Mistletoe Inn.

Chapter 16:
The Search Warrant

Gustav waited in the lobby and, right on time, Detective Chestnut arrived with her assistant, Gary, and the search warrant, which she presented to Gustav. Gustav led the two of them through each room of the inn, starting with the kitchen. Chef Marta, busy with preparations for tonight, was quite surprised to see them, but happily waited in the lobby while they searched every nook and cranny. Satisfied with their search, they told her it was complete and that she could resume her activities. She breathed a sigh of relief.

Next, they headed for the first floor rooms. Dr. Formby's was first. When they entered the room, they checked everything to make sure nothing out of the ordinary was there. The only thing they found was correspondence from the AMA, which had suspended Dr. Formby for an accusation of malpractice. That was immediately bagged as evidence. Then then moved on to Lucille Chambers' room. They found correspondence tied with a bow, all from the same person. But, what was this big book on the table? It was about foraging for mushrooms, including the poisonous ones! That was bagged as evidence as well. Next was the room of Raven Du Pree. Nothing out of the ordinary for a mystery writer was found there. Last on that floor was Scarlett Johnson's room. There they found a mortar and pestle set and immediately bagged it for evidence. Apparently, she blended essential oils as they were all over the room.

Then, they moved upstairs. First was Renata Castleberry's room. It was quite interesting because there was correspondence there as well, but from a prison! More evidence was bagged and her room searched from top to bottom. Then, the last room was that of Nancy Ellis. Her's was the saddest room. There were pictures of her and her deceased husband, pictures of her and her niece, but little else. She even had his funeral book with her. Who does that? Detective Chestnut decided there might be more to that than meets the eye so she made a note to find the cause of his death. Nancy Ellis curiously had a mistletoe plant on her table. Hmmm...also interesting.

Then, they walked back downstairs to discuss their findings. A mortar and pestle set, a book about poisonous mushrooms, and mistletoe plants in each room. Gustav did try to explain what he thought to be obvious...the name The Mistletoe Inn. But, Detective Chestnut and Gary were not amused.

The search took two hours and they were all exhausted but Detective Chestnut was interested in starting to investigate each one of the guests thoroughly to see what she could uncover. She promised Gustav an update as soon as she could determine a motive. That would only be made clear when she delved into each one of their private lives, and found out who they really were. Detective Chestnut knew that everyone kept secrets and, with the help of the Internet, many of those secrets could be exposed, possibly leading to motives for murder. That, in addition to her findings in each of their rooms, should lead to some conclusions. At least, that is what she hoped.

Detective Chestnut and Gary left the Inn by 6:45 to ensure that none of the guests saw them there. Gustav checked on the refreshments and he and Jackson brought out the grand prize for the winner of the scavenger hunt, a collection of items from shops on the historic square, which were donated by various merchants. They did not have long to wait as they heard the van arrive by 7:10. Gustav greeted them in the lobby and Jackson led them out to the fire pit for smores and hot chocolate served by Chef Marta and Bambi Lynn.

"So, did everyone have a great time?" Gustav asked. They all cheered, and seemed really happy. Gustav continued, "Who did you determine to be the winner?"

All together answered, "Scarlett."

"Great news! Scarlett! Please come here, and claim your prize!" Gustav said as he handed her the big bag of goodies from the square.

Scarlett unpacked the goodies and all the guests were impressed. There actually was quite an array of treats from the local merchants. "Now, who's ready for smores and hot chocolate?" Gustav asked. Everyone joined in, and were enjoying themselves.

Chef Marta was being praised and thanked for the delicious treats when she said, "Well, if I had known the detective was coming back, I would have made her and her assistant some."

The guests were shocked and Raven Du Pree asked, "Detective Chestnut came back?"

Gustav answered "Yes, with a search warrant for the entire inn, from top to bottom." At this, the guests appeared nervous.

Dr. Formby asked, "She searched all of our rooms?"

"Yes," replied Gustav.

Raven immediately replied, "Great! That means they now know they are dealing with a crime scene and that Mr. Fathom was indeed murdered. Now we are getting somewhere." The mood then changed immediately and, one by one, the guests excused themselves and retired to their rooms.

As Olive, Gustav, Jackson, and Chef Marta were cleaning up, Olive pulled Gustav into the office to show him something she felt important. Closing the door, she pulled out the murder board where she had placed photos of each guest and, in the middle of the board, was, of course, the deceased Mr. Fathom. She was showing Gustav this to impress him but then he shared with her the findings on the day's search. "Well, it seems several of the guests have something unusual, starting with Dr. Formby. In searching his room, we uncovered a suspension notice from the AMA due to an ongoing investigation of medical malpractice. Then, Lucille Chambers had several letters from a friend, which she bundled up. On top of the bundle was a funeral notice with an obituary. The friend had recently passed away and was, indeed, an employee of Mr. Fathom's company. She also had a book about foraging for wild mushrooms that included an entire section on poisonous ones. Scarlett Johnson's room included a picture of what appeared to be her family while she was a little girl, and then essential oils with a mortar and pestle set. Upstairs, Renata Castleberry's room had a secret as well. It seems, due to correspondence found in her room, that her husband is NOT dead, but is in prison. Last, but not least, was Nancy Ellis' room. Mrs. Ellis is a widow and she keeps his funeral book with her. Isn't that strange?"

Olive was speechless, and was writing on her murder board as fast as she could all of those facts. That gave some of the guests motives! She and Gustav hugged each other, each secretly hoping this would all be resolved the following day...and with no more deaths.

Neither Olive nor Gustav slept much that night because they now were aware that any one of their six guests could be a murderer, and one of them was most certainly! They just hoped that Detective Chestnut would solve this very quickly, and without any interaction with the press. They could not afford the negative publicity that such a scandal would bring.

Chapter 17:
Guest reactions

When Dr. Formby entered his room, he immediately saw what he feared. His suspension notice from the AMA was gone, meaning Detective Chestnut would soon know why, and would be investigating him as a prime suspect. Well, he knew that could be a possibility so would just decide how he would react when confronted with the accusations.

Lucille Chambers opened her door, saw her letters were missing, and realized they had been taken as evidence. Also, her mushroom foraging book was gone. Now, she was considered a suspect. She laid on her bed and sobbed. Not only would her friend's suicide be revealed, but now *she* was suspected of poisoning!

Scarlett entered her room to find it ransacked, her oils all gone through, and her mortar and pestle missing. How was she supposed to mix her concoctions? Then, it dawned on her. She must be the prime suspect! They would accuse her of using the oils to poison that dreadful man. She curled up in a fetal position, feeling very alone indeed.

Renata opened her door, and saw the biggest mess she had ever seen. It looked like an army had invaded her room, and overturned everything. Looking for what? She was indignant, and ready to call down and complain when she realized what was missing. The letters her husband wrote to her from prison were gone! Surely, they would not suspect *her*! How much shame could she bear? She had been so comfortable here…only to have it ruined by that odious man!

Nancy Ellis went to her room, excited by all that she had encountered and learned today. As she opened her door, she noticed nothing out of the ordinary, and decided to catch up on some reading before bed.

Chapter 18:
Renata Castleberry

Renata Castleberry was not who she seemed to be, and now was a bit put off by the murder of this guest, a Mr. Fathom. She appeared to be a rich, snobby, society widow. In reality, her husband was *not* dead, he was in prison for embezzlement from a pharmaceutical company that he'd worked for until the previous year.

Renata's husband had showered her with expensive gifts because she craved that lifestyle and, quite frankly, felt she deserved it. Renata had grown up poor. Her parents were hardworking, blue collar people. She always dreamed of living the life of the families who lived in gated communities, sent their kids to private school, and traveled the world. Her dream was coming true for a while but, last year, her husband was fired and arrested for embezzlement of company funds.

Renata was shocked, and her children mortified, and they tried to hire him a great defense team. But, that had cost more money than they had. The lawyer they hired did the best he could but, ultimately, her husband was found guilty on all counts, and sent to prison. How embarrassing that was for Renata! Her family did not have much but at least it was earned honestly. She went into a deep depression, and hardly went out after that. The kids tried to keep up with her but all she wanted to talk about was the past, and how wonderful it had been. Now, it was all gone. The attorneys let her keep some of the expensive clothes and accessories, but took all of the jewels, and anything else they determined to be bought with company funds. Renata forced herself to wear costume jewelry that looked real now. When she received this invitation, she was just certain that her husband had set this up in advance for her to enjoy the holidays. So, she arrived looking forward to a weekend where no one knew her story and where she could continue to be the wealthy socialite she always dreamed of becoming. But, now the murder was likely to bring in the press as the detective was questioning everyone! Surely, she would not make the findings public in front of the other guests, nor the innkeepers. Renata just could not bear another revealing of her real-life drama. Her husband wrote her letter after letter but she could not bring herself to visit him in prison. That was asking too much. Neither could the kids. They had seemingly moved on, and did not want him discussed at all. Hopefully, this incident would *not* make the news.

Chapter 19:
Nancy Ellis

Nancy Ellis was indeed a widow, but a recent one. She mourned her husband of forty years and, at first, locked herself away in her bungalow, not wanting any outside contact. Who could blame her? Her husband died suddenly after a drug interaction. A drug interaction to a revolutionary "cure" for male pattern baldness. Her husband had volunteered for this drug trial because he had lost his hair by age thirty, and had always been self conscious about it. He had told Nancy little about the trial because he wanted his new hair to be a surprise. No one expected it, least of all Nancy. She was horrified. She knew her husband worked for a pharmaceutical company that often had drug trials for new products. But, she had no idea that her husband was one of the trial cases. She and her husband had made plans to travel after he retired from his job but, then, suddenly, he was taken from her. No retirement and no travel. Just a funeral. Then, he was just a figure on a spreadsheet to them. The company, Live Well Pharmaceuticals, sent flowers but not one employee came to the funeral.

Nancy had no children of her own but was very close to her niece, who had become a friend to her after losing her husband. She called Nancy each week and they would go to movies sometimes, or shopping together, things that girlfriends usually do. Nancy cherished the visits and her niece also sent her gifts that she knew she would love…and she did, proudly telling everyone that her niece gave it to her. Basically, Nancy became a new woman when she had someone to do things with again.

That is why she was certain that her niece was spoiling her with this weekend at The Mistletoe Inn. Her only regret was that her niece did not come with her. Her niece denied sending it, and seemed puzzled by who could have sent it, but Nancy knew in her heart it was her. Who knew? Maybe she would find a new friend here. After all, there were others traveling alone as well. But, the murder of Mr. Fathom was something totally unexpected. Nancy had never experienced anything like this before. Now, as the detective was questioning everyone, she became more wary of the other guests. She did not know any of these people. Were they capable of murder? Who knew?

Chapter 20:
Bambi Lynn

What a day! Bambi Lynn went home, and immediately poured herself a strong drink. She had never experienced a day like this before. She thought she had seen it all from her days as an exotic dancer. Sleazy customers, sleazy employers, and girls that simply did not care.

When Bambi decided to leave that world behind, and make a new start, she cleaned up her act, looked presentable, and applied for the first job that came along - a maid for this beautiful bed and breakfast. It had only seven rooms total, and was normally not full. She certainly had house cleaning experience and she had no criminal record. The owners seemed so nice, and were so much nicer than the strip club owners. She also got along with Chef Marta and Jackson just fine. It seemed like the perfect job to her because she was home every day by 4:00 and that gave her time to work on her online associates degree in hospitality. With that, she could get a job in any hotel as a front desk clerk, or even an event person. She loved special events, and often volunteered to help with any booked at the inn.

But, today was different. She never thought she would be up close and personal with a dead body like that! What a shock! She was trying to get the image out of her mind but, every time she closed her eyes, there he was! Now there was an active investigation at the inn. Who knew what that could turn up? Who killed him? She had certainly worked around unsavory characters before, but not murderers...at least not to her knowledge.

Now, she had to try and get some rest before facing the guests again the following day. At least that was their last full day but they would still be in and out all day, going to the special event planned for that evening, and then, the next morning, they would check out. It would take all the courage she could raise to not be suspicious, and afraid of all of them.

Chapter 21:
Detective Chestnut

Detective Sara Chestnut was a relatively new member of the Jeffersonville Police Force, having come from neighboring Mayfield where she was in charge of the jail and the warrant division, working closely with the sheriff. She was single so she'd had plenty of time to learn from him, and study the book for her dream job as a detective. She took the detective exam, and applied for the job to expand her law enforcement career and now she was under fire to find this killer! Who kills someone at a Christmas themed weekend at a bed and breakfast? After she and her assistant, Gary, completed the search of all of the guest rooms, she was simply amazed. Each guest was hiding something…except that mystery writer. It was either just a crazy set of coincidences, or a set up for murder. At that point, she could not say which. Sara really did not believe in coincidences but this could be the work of a calculated killer. She did not sleep well that night as all the details kept running through her mind. Was she missing something?

Chapter 22:
The Next Day

At breakfast the guests were quieter than normal, and more reserved. Gustav and Olive tried to lighten the mood by chatting with all of the guests, and reminding them of the special event that evening, with surprise entertainment straight from Las Vegas. Chef Marta was preparing a wonderful meal and it was to be a stellar evening for everyone.

Immediately after breakfast, Raven Du Pree approached Gustav, and asked him if he thought Detective Chestnut would like her help with the case. "It certainly couldn't hurt," replied Gustav. He offered to drive her to the police station, and take her in to see the detective. She agreed and off they went.

At the station, Detective Chestnut actually was happy to see Raven because she was totally overwhelmed with several leads to follow, things to check on, and pieces to put together. Raven started sharing the information she had found on the Internet, along with some personal insights she had gleaned from the guests themselves. They went, guest by guest, over every detail. That took quite a while because they researched each guest's background, any ties they might have with the deceased, and any possible motive they could have had. There were many! Even Raven was shocked to find out what secrets each guest was hiding. They worked until almost 4:00 and then Gary, Detective Chestnut's assistant, drove Raven back to The Mistletoe Inn so that she had plenty of time to get ready for the festive evening ahead, which was certainly going to be memorable for all the guests and the staff alike.

At the inn, Chef Marta had been working feverishly to make sure everything was going to be perfect to serve the guests as this was their last event and she wanted it to be the most elegant banquet they had ever attended. Plus, she also was trying to go above and beyond to prove herself beyond suspicion in all of the investigation business.

Bambi Lynn was setting all the tables in the dining room, placing all the florals on each table, and making sure that every detail was taken care of to the highest standard. She was nervous because there was a kind of tension in the air, with everyone looking askance at everyone else to try to determine who could have committed this murder.

Olive and Gustav were making sure the evening plans were going to be flawless, even down to the music selections. They wanted this to be the final memory for the guests. Olive had a beautiful, emerald green dress for the night and Gustav put on his Christmas tie, just to be more festive with his suit. Even Jackson was festive, wearing a Christmas plaid vest with his suit. They had no idea what was about to happen. Detective Chestnut and Raven did not share with them their findings, and wanted to keep tonight's reveal a complete surprise for everyone. Were they nervous? Of course, because so much was riding on this weekend to help keep the inn afloat. Olive was trying not to be emotional but Gustav could tell that she was very nervous indeed. Just before it was time to go and greet the guests, they hugged and Gustav promised her that everything was going to be alright. He told her he felt that this evening was going to be so unique that the guests would not ever forget it. Little did he know how true that would be!

The guests were also in fine form for the special evening. Dr. Formby was in a tuxedo, looking quite dapper, with a Christmas bow tie for his nod to the holiday.

Lucille Chambers was in a lovely red dress, and carrying a jeweled evening bag, which had been a present from her friend Alice last Christmas.

Scarlett was dressed in a black velvet, off the shoulder dress. Her only decoration was a beautiful locket around her neck.

The next to arrive was Nancy Ellis, dressed in a shimmering white pants outfit. She wore a lovely Christmas pin on the lapel, and carried a silver and white shawl around her shoulders.

Raven arrived next in a beautifully tailored suit with strands of pearls around her neck. Professional yet elegant would be the description of her outfit.

Last, but certainly not least, Renata made quite an entrance! She wore a sequined blue dress, with a beautiful lapis necklace, and chandelier earrings. Wow! She could not help but notice all eyes on her as she found her seat and, of course, asked for a champagne cocktail.

Chapter 23:
The Banquet

At promptly 7:00, the guests were all seated in the beautifully decorated dining room, having cocktails and appetizers while chatting about the evening. Gustav and Olive were excited about the evening's entertainment surprise and just could not wait any longer!

Gustav started, "Welcome everyone! We are so happy you are here, and hope you have been enjoying all of the holiday events that we planned for you." All the guests applauded and he continued "Now, to top it all off, straight from Las Vegas, please welcome, Elvis!"

Gasps came from the guests as an Elvis impersonator took the stage and began singing "Blue Christmas." The guests loved it and they were all singing along, even Dr. Formby. They did not even notice when Detective Chestnut, Gary, and two other officers arrived.

When "Elvis" finished his set, the guests all gave him a standing ovation and that was when they began to notice the detective and the other officers in the room.

Gustav spoke, "We are so happy we could bring you this level of entertainment to end the weekend on a high that would surprise everyone!"

Detective Chestnut then took the floor, "You got that right, Mr. Boudreaux! Everyone will be surprised to hear what I have found out, I can assure you! Now, everyone please be seated as I enlighten you on my findings."

Olive Boudreaux had slipped out during this first part. She then came back with her murder board, and showed the detective. "This may help you…" she said.

Detective Chestnut replied, "Oh, yes! This is exactly what we need."

The guests were all nervous when they saw the board with Mr. Fathom's picture in the center, and all of their pictures surrounding his.

Chapter 24
A Murderer is Revealed

Detective Chestnut began, "While you were all out on the scavenger hunt, we came with a search warrant, and went through each room in this inn. The findings were actually remarkable. All of you have things to hide, things that are now found out, and that might hold a bearing on this case. In case you did not know, Mr. Fathom was poisoned by mistletoe berries."

Gasps erupted from the guests, except for Raven du Pree. Detective Chestnut continued, "It seems the poison was administered in his soda but that alone did not kill him." Everyone gasped again.

"No, he was smothered after he was poisoned. It seems the poison was not enough. Maybe he did not drink enough. It's hard to say but we found the residue on the pillow case, so it was the pillow that finished him off. As to what brought all of you here for this weekend, with the exception of Raven Du Pree, you were all invited by Mr. Fathom's lawyer, Jeff Willingham." Gasps were heard across the tables. "That is correct. He invited all of you, and prepaid for you under the name Blue Skies Investments with the hopes of Mr. Fathom interacting with you, and making amends to each one of you. You see, we now know he had wronged each one of you, as we will now discuss. His uncle, Ben Cooper, had charged him with the task of making these amends to each of you before it was too late. Unfortunately, one of you took matters into your own hands and he was unable to accomplish this task," said Detective Chestnut.

Now, as to each of you, starting with Dr. Formby, you, sir, are *not* here on a break. You are under suspension of your license due to a medical malpractice hearing being investigated now. It seems you failed to diagnose a patient's cancer and she died. Her fiancée was none other than Mr. Fathom!"

Everyone turned to stare at Dr. Formby, who just looked down at his plate. Raven Du Pree got up from her seat, and joined the Detective. "What do you have to say about that, Doctor?" asked Detective Chestnut.

"I did not know him per se. I knew *of him*, certainly, especially when he filed that complaint against me," Dr. Formby replied in his defense. "I had never seen him before," he continued. "I treated her for the symptoms that she had, which are common for acid reflux. Never in my practice had I seen anyone with those symptoms who had esophageal cancer. I certainly would have done many more tests had her symptoms warranted that. But, I had no reason to kill Fathom. The complaint was already filed and they had suspended me until the investigation would be completed. Killing him would not change any of this. I will have to live with that mistake for the rest of my life, believe me. I knew better than to try and confront him as it probably would hurt my case."

Detective Chestnut continued, "Next, we have Lucille Chambers. A sweet little lady who recently lost a very close friend who committed suicide after constant verbal assaults and abuse by her employer, Mr. Fathom. Lucille was also an avid forager of mushrooms, and has quite extensive knowledge of poisonous ones as well. Ms. Chambers, what have you to say about this?"

Ms. Chambers rose from her chair, and replied, "I had no idea who Mr. Fathom was until someone mentioned his company, Live Well Pharmaceuticals. Then, I certainly knew who he was, and could understand why he was such a loner. No one would want to be friends with someone like that. But, I certainly did not kill him. I confess to staring at him that first morning at breakfast, trying to understand why he wanted no contact with anyone. Now, I completely understand. He drove my friend Alice to a complete mental breakdown. I tried and tried to get her to leave the company, and find another job, but she felt like she had to stay to watch over things, and try to help the clients who were having issues with the drugs they were making. She kept trying to get him to schedule more trials, and wait until they had enough data to safely launch the drugs. But, he wanted to rush them out to be the first to launch. It was like a sick game to him." By that point Lucille was crying and she needed a hand to help her back into her seat.

Detective Chestnut continued, "And, then we have Miss Scarlett Johnson, so young and innocent, but hiding quite the secret. You see, Miss Johnson is all alone because she lost both her parents in a horrible accident years ago due to a drunk driver who had his lawyer get him community service. That man was Nigel Fathom."

Everyone looked shocked except for Scarlett. She answered, "I had never seen him until that first morning at breakfast. I, too, was staring at him, wondering if it ever crossed his mind that he took *everything* from me! He never admitted his guilt, and never said a word. He just let his lawyer handle it and I lost my world because of him! I knew his name, and had attempted to contact him before but he never answered me. He clearly did not care about me, or what he had taken from me." At that point, Scarlett was weeping and Dr. Formby helped her back into her seat.

Detective Chestnut continued, "Only one of you did not have anything to hide, or an ulterior motive. That was Raven Du Pree. She is exactly who she says, a famous mystery writer and, I must say, she was quite valuable to me today, helping to piece together exactly what happened to Mr. Fathom." Raven just nodded, and kept her spot next to the detective.

Detective Chestnut continued, "Renata Castleberry...now here is a shocker for you. she is *not* a widow at all. Her husband is currently serving time in prison for embezzlement from Live Well Pharmaceuticals. Yes, that's right...Mr. Fathom's company. You have all been noticing her expensive clothing and accessories. Well, now you know."

Renata jumped up, and exclaimed, "That is a lie! My husband was innocent! Those were bonuses he was promised, but was never given. He was just taking what he was owed. Fathom's team of lawyers just buried my husband and we did not have the funds to compete with them so he was convicted. I had no idea who the man was until someone mentioned his name. Then, I certainly knew it was him. He took everything from me! My children will not visit, the embarrassment from the community, and my life basically ended when he was convicted. But, did I kill him? No, I did *not*! I would have had no idea how to poison anyone." Renata finished, and sat down with a glare at the detective.

"Let's see, who does that leave? Well, Nancy Ellis. Mrs. Ellis is indeed a widow. That part is true. She lost her husband to a strange drug interaction in a drug trial at Live Well Pharmaceuticals, Mr. Fathom's company. Apparently, that drug was rushed to market, and should have had more research trials but Mr. Ellis took the drug voluntarily, not having any idea of its toxicity. He died within 30 days of the drug trial. Mrs. Ellis was given a small settlement to keep quiet about the cause of death, but that should have triggered a large-scale investigation into the company's drug release practices, and the records of any and all drug tests given. Mrs. Ellis, we are very sorry for your loss. Do you have anything to say?" asked Detective Chestnut.

Mrs. Ellis just stayed in her seat, looking down, and replied, "No, detective. I miss my husband every day. Am I angry about his dying due to a drug interaction? Of *course*! But, he was such a kind man. He would never want me to seek revenge. My niece has comforted me so much, and kept up with me, I am doing okay with being alone. Not great, just okay. This holiday weekend seemed just what I needed to brighten up my life but I certainly had no idea that *he* would be here. Of course, I knew his name. I, too, stared at him, and even went over and tried to talk with him that first morning but he would not even acknowledge me...even when I told him my name. I admit I cried over that. He did not even seem to recognize the name. I do not want my husband's death to be in vain. I want people to know how deadly that drug can be. Did I poison him? Of course not! I admit to having mistletoe in my room but that is because it is everywhere here and I thought it went with the theme of the weekend," she finished, and dabbed at her eyes.

Detective Chestnut continued, "No, you did not poison him, Mrs. Ellis, but someone certainly did and that someone was..."

Raven interrupted the detective. "I got this. All of you lost someone or something very important because of Mr. Fathom but the murderer suffered the greatest loss of all. Miss Scarlett Johnson, please stand up. Mr. Fathom took away your childhood and your chance of a normal family life because he was driving the car that hit and killed both your parents that terrible evening. Not only that but he was driving intoxicated. He was very impaired, it was raining, and it was a horrible crime for sure. He had his lawyer cover it up as best he could, with making payments to make sure your basic needs were taken care of financially. But, he never admitted to you that he was the driver, nor that he was sorry. At the tree trimming party, you slipped away for a few minutes to place the poison juice in his soda, conveniently sitting outside his door. You then hurried back down to join everyone else so that, hopefully, no one would notice. How did you get the juice? Well, a mortar and pestle set were found in your room and the residue was still there as per the lab report."

At this point, Scarlett started weeping, and said, "Yes, that man took *everything* from me! He never one time had to say he was sorry, or even admit he did anything wrong. When I heard his name on the first day, I knew I had to confront him but he would not even make eye contact with me. That is when I *knew* I could not let this go on any longer. Yes, I travel with a mortar and pestle set to work on my essential oil blends so it was no big deal to extract the poison from the berries, put it in a vial, and slip it into his glass."

Detective Chestnut interrupted, "But, that wasn't enough, was it Miss Scarlett? You had to finish him off later."

Miss Scarlett replied, "Well, yes, I did check on him late in the night. It was very easy to gain entrance to his room with an ordinary credit card. I had to be sure of him being out but, to my surprise, he was still alive. Weak, but alive. He did not finish his soda. Therefore, he did not get enough of the poison so I spoke to him to give him one more chance to apologize, which he would not do. Then, I just helped him along by holding a pillow over his face. He fought a bit, coughing and wheezing, but he was already weak so it did not take long. I wish I was sorry but not really. He deserved it, and *now* that I know the other people he wronged, he certainly *did* deserve it."

Gary, who was standing behind Miss Scarlett, started reading her rights, and placed her in handcuffs.

Detective Chestnut thanked Raven for all of her help, and promised to read some of her books. She and Gary then took Miss Scarlett out to the car to transport her to jail.

Gustav and Olive faced the other guests, and tried to end the evening on a lighter note by thanking them all for coming, and telling them they would be honored to have them come again for a stay. The other guests are mumbling to themselves, doubtful they would ever return to The Mistletoe Inn, but admitting they would never forget this weekend.

One by one, they filed out, heading to their rooms. Gustav, Olive, and Jackson prepared to clean up.

They quietly cleaned up while worrying about the fate of the inn due to the publicity that most certainly would ensue now that a murder had taken place here. How bad would it be? Would their reputation be salvageable after this? As Gustav and Olive retired to their suite, physically tired, and in need of sleep, worry kept them from their much needed rest.

Chapter 25:
Guest Reactions

Dr. Formby could not wait to get to his room, and collapse on the bed. What a night! Who could have predicted the outcome of that investigation? The relief that soon came over him was enough to lull him to sleep, but with troubled dreams...

Lucille Chambers started crying as soon as she entered her room. Oh, the terrible things revealed tonight! She decided she would do something positive in Alice's memory when she got home. What an awful man her boss was! No wonder she was so miserable there! She fell asleep thinking of ways to remember her sweet friend.

Raven was typing away. She lost a day of work helping Detective Chestnut solve the case so she would need to pull an all nighter to catch up. The deadline her publisher had set was indeed looming but she was invigorated at the solving of the murder so she did not mind as she was in the zone.

Renata was simply broken. She could not get to her room fast enough, and lock the door. Yet again, her secrets had been revealed like dirty laundry to all the other guests. Good riddance to that horrible man! *That girl did us all a favor*, thought Renata. Her mind started working and she just could not sleep because all of the bad thoughts just kept coming.

Nancy Ellis was very sad as she closed her door. That poor girl Scarlett. Now, she would never condone what she did. After all, murder is murder. But, she knew he was a miserable excuse for a human being after hearing all of those misdeeds, and using a lawyer to escape justice. The saddest thing of all was that none of this would bring back her husband. Nancy cried herself to sleep.

Chapter 26:
Breakfast

The next morning, breakfast was served in the dining room and the mood was somber, to say the least. All the guests were now aware that they shared a common interest or painful memory that was now exposed to everyone. Their lives would never be the same again.

Attorney Jeff Willingham came into the dining room, and asked Gustav if he could address the guests. Gustav reluctantly agreed, worried about their reactions to what news he had come to share with them.

Jeff held envelopes in his right hand. He began, "My name is Jeff Willingham. I am the attorney for the recently deceased Ben Cooper, the uncle of Mr. Fathom, whom you all have had unfortunate dealings with in one way or another. You were invited here at Mr. Cooper's request in the hopes that Mr. Fathom would make amends to you, or at least try to do so. Unfortunately, that did not happen and now he has passed as well. He was the only heir to Mr. Cooper's fortune. This presents quite the conundrum as Mr. Fathom also had no heirs…so what will happen with the inheritance? Mr. Cooper had a provision in his will that stated each of you were to be compensated for your losses. While we realize that money cannot bring back loved ones or a reputation, it can offer a second chance, a new beginning, or even perhaps a new locale. I have envelopes with generous amounts for each of you. Please accept them with heartfelt sympathy from Mr. Cooper over your losses, and how you were treated by Mr. Fathom."

One by one, the guests came up to receive their envelopes, and then silently retreated to their rooms, after acknowledging Mr.

Willingham's genuine concern. All except for Renata Castleberry, who seemed furious!

"You expect this, whatever it is, to repay my loss? My husband is still in prison because of *you*, my children will have nothing to do with me, my friends have deserted me, and my life is in ruins," she exclaimed. She stormed out of the room before Jeff could come up with an attorney answer. He made a mental note to check into her situation, and see if there was any reason for her to feel such anger.

When Renata got to her room, she sobbed on the bed. She did, indeed, feel ruined. No envelope was going to change that. What could she do? She needed her children around her at a time like this. Maybe if she called them, they would know what to do. She made a plan to contact them and then, together, they would plan their next move.

Chapter 27:
Check Out Time

As time for the guests to check out approached, Olive and Gustav became more nervous than ever! They simply could not withstand all the bad press that surely would follow. They did nothing wrong! Olive and Gustav held each other tightly before going to the lobby to perform their usual task of saying a final goodbye to each guest personally, and making sure to do two things: Invite them to stay again, and ask them to consider leaving a Google review as they were a small business, and every review counted.

Raven was the first to leave, and promised to leave a review as soon as she got her research completed, as well as help solve another case in Texas. She thanked both Olive and Gustav for their hospitality, and for the holiday themed weekend.

Next was Lucille Chambers. She also thanked Olive and Gustav for the holiday activities, and promised to post a review herself. She said that she planned to use the money for a memorial for her friend, and also to establish a fund for mental health group retreats so her friend's death would not be in vain.

Dr. Formby was next. He shook Gustav's hand, tipped his hat to Olive, and promised to write a review when he returned home. He seemed more at ease than when he arrived, and felt like he could survive the suspension after this weekend. He vowed to use his money to promote more cancer screenings and early detection in his small town.

Nancy Ellis came down next, and was ever so gracious, hugging both Gustav and Olive, and thanking them for the wonderful holiday-themed events. She would get her niece to help her write a review because she had never done one before. She also told them she was going to use her money to travel, solo and with her niece, as she wanted to experience more of life now; no longer locking herself away with her grief.

Lastly, Renata came down. She barely looked at Gustav and Olive. When they spoke to her about coming back to The Mistletoe Inn, she broke down in tears, and simply said, "No! Too many bad memories here." Then, over her shoulder, she exclaimed, "You have not heard the last of me. Mark my words!"

When she was out of sight, Gustav and Olive were simply shattered. What did she mean by that? Why was she angry with them? They did not murder anyone, nor accuse anyone of anything. Olive began to weep and Gustav had to help her to their suite. Gustav tried to reassure Olive that Renata's anger was just misfocused. She was not angry at them, but at the situation. He decided to investigate her situation privately, and see if she had any reason to feel as if she were wronged.

Chapter 28:
Jeff Willingham

When Jeff left The Mistletoe Inn, he immediately headed towards home. But, instead of feeling relieved after giving out the monies to the five guests, he was indeed troubled by Renata's reaction and angry words. From what he remembered, her husband was clearly guilty of embezzling funds from Live Well Pharmaceuticals and there was not much the defense could do or say to alleviate the charges. He tried to remember as much as he could about the trial to see if they, indeed, completely buried him to the point where where only a high-powered defense could save him. But, really, theft was theft, especially at that level. Apparently, it had been happening for some time before they caught it. Now, as to the allegations that he was owed those funds, he would certainly check into that the following morning. Oh, he most certainly was not looking forward to that. Now they would have to completely restructure the company and he would have to be in charge of that, as per the instructions left him by Mr. Fathom's will. Once again, his family would suffer as he would certainly be burning the midnight oil as the Interim CEO until all could be resolved.

How would the employees react? There would probably mixed feelings as Nigel Fathom was not well liked at all, but also fear of who would take his place, the restructuring process, and of some possibly losing their jobs. He also needed to put individuals in place to assure that *no* more drugs were rushed to market and *no* more drug trials would be performed until all the side effects were carefully weighed, and all the FDA standards were met.

He decided to take his wife out to dinner, and try to explain what these events would mean to their family for the next few months.

Also, the board would need to hold an emergency meeting as soon as possible to go over the search criteria for the new management, as well as enlightening them on the activities of the previous weekend.

As he kept driving, Jeff could feel the pressure mounting on him. He finally pulled over to have a quick lunch, hoping that would help his mood. He was halfway home but needed a break. He called home to tell his wife of his progress, and gave her an estimated time of his arrival.

Chapter 29:
Detective Chestnut

Detective Chestnut was feeling much better now that she had solved the murder case with the help of Raven DuPree. And, she was starting to plan some holiday activities herself. Being single in that small town did not present many opportunities for dating, but certainly did give her many invitations to join this family or that one for their celebrations. Also, the downtown square offered many holiday activities as well. Maybe that Christmas would be the start of establishing new traditions that she could enjoy. First things first, though, she would need to focus on the trial of Scarlett Johnson.

She would contact the court on Monday to set a date for her indictment hearing. That should be quite quick since she had already admitted to killing him. Then, the jury selection would begin. This would be, hopefully, a quick trial as the guilt was already agreed upon. However, she was planning on the jury being sympathetic to her situation and, instead of murder one, maybe the defendant would get a lesser charge, with a much lighter sentence. Scarlett had used her one phone call to contact a lawyer, and met with her, an unknown to Detective Chestnut. But, that lawyer, Robert Blake, seemed quite capable of representing Scarlett well. Maybe a phone call to attorney Jeff Willingham would be in order as well. After all, if he defended the deceased Mr. Fathom in the case of the killing of both of her parents in a horrible drunk driving accident, then those facts would most certainly come up in her defense. If he avoided justice by any means other than a technicality, etc., then that could prove to be the catalyst to reduce or even drop her charges. Maybe she should research his law career as well.

Detective Chestnut also made a point of researching Raven Du Pree's books, and ordered a couple on Amazon. She felt it couldn't hurt to read how those fictional characters solved murders, especially since she had been so impressed with Raven's insight and research into the murder at The Mistletoe Inn.

Detective Chestnut hoped that all the negative publicity that the murder, and subsequent trial, would bring would not ruin Gustav and Olive because they were probably struggling as it was. Maybe she would recommend them to anyone she knew who was looking for a venue for a special event. She was determined to try because she certainly did not want them to fail.

Chapter 30:
Staff Plans after Check out

As Bambi Lynn was cleaning all the guest rooms, there was an eerie quiet all through the house. She expected this so she turned up her music on her playlist, and tried to forget all that had happened during the previous few days. When she got to the room where the murder had happened, she shuddered as she changed the bed, and used extra cleaners on all the other surfaces to erase any traces of the former guest, and the police investigation.

She knew she would feel much better when that day was over and the next round of guests appeared. Only then could she hope to erase the bad feelings associated with that room. As a final touch, she sprayed fresh linen spray to help freshen the room as well.

Jackson was off that day, and was enjoying himself with a group of friends, until talk of the murder surfaced and he found himself the center of attention with everyone wanting all the grisly details. He tried to be as tightlipped as possible since he knew that they could not sustain any bad publicity. He eventually managed to change the subject to everyone's holiday plans and then he was able to relax.

Chef Marta was also off after cleaning up breakfast so she was spending the time with her family. Caring for her mom and her teens was her priority that day, as well as relaxing. She tried to focus on their own Christmas tree, and decorating it as a family. What a week at work! She certainly did not want to have to go through that again! She did feel sorry for Gustav and Olive. They were such good people and she knew they were struggling.

Back at the inn, Gustav was in his office while Olive was taking a nap. He was thankful everyone was gone and that it was quiet again so he could think. Of course, he could think of little else than the previous few days. What would everything mean for their upcoming business? Would publicity be as bad as he feared, especially with the impending trial of Scarlett Johnson, the young, innocent looking girl who had committed murder by poison, and by suffocation? Maybe they could plan some holiday events for the town before the trial began. Yes, that was a great idea. Maybe caroling and cookies. He would mention this at the upcoming staff meeting tomorrow, and then call the downtown association, and invite them. The inn still looked beautiful from all the decorations so maybe that would help their image with the townspeople.

Then, he took a look at the upcoming reservations online and, to his surprise, there were several. Not totally full, but enough to keep them going for a while. Gustav bowed his head, and thanked God for that blessing. At last, there was some good news for himself, Olive, and the staff.

Chapter 31:
Renata

Renata was so distraught when she left The Mistletoe Inn that her eyes kept filling with tears. She had called her boys to tell them she was on her way home, and desperately needed to see them. Neither answered so she was forced to leave frantic messages for each of them. She wanted them to hear what had happened, and orchestrate a plan to sue Live Well Pharmaceuticals, especially with all her new information on their misdeeds. They would simply need a good lawyer and, with all the new information, surely someone would take their case.

She was driving erratically because she was so upset. She could not see clearly, and missed her turn. Before she knew it, she was headed across the bridge over Caddo Lake. It was cold, foggy, and rainy, which did not make the visibility any better and, when she crossed the bridge, intending to turn around, and go back the other way, she felt a big bump and her car slid off the road, down the embankment.

It all happened so fast! Her car slid into the lake, shrouded by all the mossy cypress trees and, just minutes later, she found herself submerged in the murky water. She tried to call for help but no one could hear her as her car slid under the water in less than three minutes. The cold weather in December, plus the rain and foggy conditions, made for an empty shoreline. Renata was strong for her age, and tried valiantly to escape the rising water in the car but, eventually, it was all too much for her. Renata did not know that underneath the bridge was the deepest part of the

Sheila Williamson

lake, and the most deadly, and that the water was very swift moving.

Chapter 32: Caddo Lake

Caddo Lake spans 25,400 acres, and is situated on the state line between Texas and Louisiana. It is the largest naturally formed lake in Texas, and boasts the largest flooded bald cypress forest in the world.

The lake was formed naturally but a dam was added for flood control and other purposes. That area is steeped in history for its formation, and for the Caddo people.

Caddo Lake's waters can be hazardous, with strong currents, and many submerged obstacles.

The average depth of Caddo Lake is 4.6 feet with deeper water covering more than 50 percent of the lake-surface area. The greatest depth is located in the eastern part of the lake just east of the Highway 538 bridge where the water depth is approximately 27 feet.

Alligators do live in and around Caddo Lake and there are posted warnings everywhere. Snapping turtles and strange shark-like paddlefish, the oldest species in North America, also are permanent residents there.

Caddo Lake is known for its eerie and mysterious atmosphere, particularly at night, which has inspired numerous ghost stories and legends. The lake's unique landscape of cypress trees draped in Spanish moss, coupled with its history of accidents and folklore, contribute to its spooky reputation.

Chapter 33:
Monday

Gustav and Olive were ready for that week's staff meeting. Gustav was looking forward to sharing his new idea. Jackson, Chef Marta, and Bambi Lynn all made their way to the lobby where they were greeted with smiles and a handout to explain Gustav's new idea.

As they sat, Gustav explained, "The idea came to me yesterday in the quiet after everyone had gone. What better way to boost our positive image than to invite the downtown merchants to a caroling and cookies party?"

The staff nodded and Chef Marta spoke first, "I will be happy to make cookies, and maybe other treats to make this special. I think we should invite Detective Chestnut and her assistant, Gary, as well. Don't you think?"

Olive was not so sure about that, but decided to stay quiet. Gustav answered her, "Yes, I think that is a grand idea. More goodwill goes a long way towards healing."

Bambi Lynn and Jackson both agreed to help in any way. They looked at the calendar, and settled upon a date. Jackson offered to make up flyers and Gustav would distribute them the following day at the Chamber of Commerce meeting, and around the square.

"Now, let's look at our calendar of reservations for this upcoming week, shall we?" Gustav mentioned the next group arriving was on Thursday, and leaving Sunday. "Let's do ornament making on Thursday night, Friday night game night, and, on Saturday, let's do an ugly Christmas sweater contest with entertainment.

Jackson, can you possibly get that local group from the winery to perform for our guests?" Jackson wrote that on his to-do list, and agreed.

Olive said, "For the game night, I found a great Christmas trivia game. Can we please try that?" They all agreed it sounded like fun and she was happy to facilitate that idea.

Chef Marta was busily writing all of the events down, and said, "I can do cookies and hot chocolate for the ornament making, pizza for the game night, and a pasta night for the ugly sweater contest, with the dessert being ugly sweater decorated cookies. Does that sound okay?" Gustav heartily agreed and Chef Marta started forming her grocery list.

Bambi Lynn asked, "What ornaments were you planning on making? I have a couple of ideas I could show you that I have done before." Gustav and Olive both loved that idea. This took Bambi Lynn's mind off all the negativity of last week and then she had something positive to focus on. They had a couple of days to formulate all these plans, and to get their to-do lists in order before any guests arrived.

All in all, it was a great staff meeting, and a positive start to the new week.

Then, the phone rang...

Chapter 34:
Live Well Pharmaceuticals

As Jeff made his way into the building, he was greeted by the receptionist, who informed him the board was awaiting his arrival. He made his way to the conference room, and thought to himself, *now it begins*.

The board members were all gathered around the table, awaiting his direction since he was the only one who knew all the contents of Nigel Fathom's will, and, more than that, the other events that had transpired over the years that he had kept secret due to attorney/client privilege.

He began with going over the events at The Mistletoe Inn, the purpose of the stay, the people involved, and, one-by-one, the wrongs that had been committed. He concluded by going over the amounts that each had been given, except for Scarlett Johnson, who was currently in the Jacksonville jail, awaiting arraignment, which was to take place that day.

The board members were sufficiently shocked and disgusted by some of what he had to say. Others were very sad, and even nervously anticipating what was to come next.

Next was the reading of the portion of the will that included Live Well Pharmaceuticals. It was stipulated that Jeff himself was to be in charge until a suitable CEO could be found with the approval of the board. A sigh of relief went over them when this was read as it certainly would give them a chance to turn things around. To add to that, Jeff read to them the portion of Ben Fathom's trust, which addressed what would occur in the case of the death of his nephew, Nigel. It made things crystal clear that the business would now be completely above board with no more rushing drugs to market, falsifying test results, etc. At that time, Jeff paused, and asked for questions or comments.

The board gave him a complete vote of confidence and then their only question was their possible upcoming involvement in the murder trial. Jeff assured them the company would bear no burden in the trial as this was a personal matter between Scarlett and Nigel Fathom. It did not involve the company.

However, he would probably be involved as a witness for the prosecution since he was Nigel's lawyer. He explained that he simply did as he was told many years ago by Ben Fathom. On this day, he regretted that decision as Scarlett was robbed of a childhood by that one decision.

The board wanted him to apprise them of the hearing and subsequent trial to which he heartily agreed. They also wanted to know if the company bore any further legal obligations to Dr. Formby, the family of Alice who committed suicide, or to the widow Nancy Ellis? Jeff reminded them of the envelopes, which were generous settlements, and did not think anything else was necessary.

Now, as for Renata, the wife of the person in prison for embezzlement, Jeff honestly told them how vengeful she was to the detective and to him. He also promised to look carefully at that case to be sure that it was all above board, and that nothing was done that could be construed as wrong on the company's part.

At that point, the board meeting was adjourned and it was decided that a slate of potential candidates would be discussed at the next meeting set for the following Monday, in hopes of filling the position by January 1.

Next, Jeff needed to address the employees. He had the receptionist call all the department managers, and have them report to the conference room at noon, with sandwiches to be delivered so that they would not miss lunch. Maybe all the news would go down a bit easier.

Jeff's phone started ringing and he looked down. It was coming from an unknown number. He answered and it was Detective Chestnut. She was calling to inform him that, indeed, Scarlett had been indicted for murder and her trial date was set for January 15 to give her attorney plenty of time to research the past situation that led to this act. She was remanded in their custody so she would be in the Jeffersonville jail until that date. Jeff thanked the detective, and offered any help he could give. The detective assured him he probably would be called as a witness for the defense since he was Fathom's attorney at the time. That was just what he had feared. He would definitely be researching the facts himself so as not to be blindsided in court. He thanked her for calling.

Jeff entered the conference room where all of the managers were gathered, and went through the events leading up to Mr. Fathom's death. He then told them the board was researching candidates to lead the company and that it was going to change the way business was done. No longer were drugs to be rushed to market, nor any records falsely reported. It was going to be an open, honest business that operated to live up to its name, Live Well. They were going to value their employees, and he tasked each manager to report to him their employees, how long they had been there, the last time they were reviewed, and the raises that were deserved. That would be discussed with the board, as well as Christmas bonuses, which they had never received before.

The managers were ecstatic! They knew things would change, but had no idea it would be that positive. They could hardly wait to get the message to their people. They all shook Jeff's hand as they exited and he breathed a sigh of relief.

Then, to research the mess with Castleberry... He needed to find the file in HR, and then sit down, and absorb it. Could she possibly be right? Surely not...

Chapter 35:
Scarlett's Hearing

On Monday morning, Scarlett Johnson was arraigned in the courtroom of Judge Candace Owen. Her attorney was present and he approached the bench, as did the prosecutor. He told the judge that, due to extenuating circumstances, the confession made was not admissible and Scarlett wished to have a jury trial. The prosecutor was shocked, and said, "Your Honor, this is an open and shut case. She admitted guilt in front of many witnesses."

Judge Owen asked what the circumstances were and the attorney simply said, "Past occurrences that have driven this action, and that there were many suspects that had motive and opportunity in the inn, as well as her. Miss Johnson feels this will all come out in a trial of her peers so that all will be fair."

The judge contemplated for a moment, and then ruled that Scarlett be remanded to the jail while discovery was to be made. The trial date was set for January 15, after the holidays.

Chapter 36:
The Phone Call

Back at The Mistletoe Inn, the phone rang and Jackson answered. It was a young man inquiring about the former guest, Renata Castleberry. Jackson answered that she had checked out on Sunday, and left in her car. The young man informed Jackson that Renata had called him and his brother both on Sunday, frantic to speak to them about events that had happened at the inn. They were to meet her at her home but she never arrived. He wanted to know what she meant by the events that had happened, what went on during her stay, and what kind of place was the inn? He was getting more and more upset so Jackson did the right thing, and got Gustav to speak to him.

Gustav answered, "Hello, this is the owner of The Mistletoe Inn. What may I help you with?"

The son responded, retelling about Renata's message on Sunday, and asking all the same questions. What did she mean by the events that had happened at the inn? What went on during her stay? What kind of place was that? And, most importantly, where was Renata now?

Gustav answered the most diplomatically her could. "She left the inn on Sunday, presumably to go home, and have not seen nor heard from her since then. The events were a tree trimming party, a scavenger hunt, and a banquet with entertainment attended by all the guests as that was our special holiday-themed weekend.

He added, "Unfortunately, there was an incident that occurred with one of the guests who was found deceased but it was handled professionally and quickly by the local law enforcement.

No other guests were ever in any danger. The perpetrator was apprehended, and is jailed, awaiting trial."

The son, Charles Castleberry, was incredulous at this report. "You mean to tell me that there was a *murder* at your inn while my mother was a guest, and that the activities continued on? Who does that? Why was the inn not immediately declared a crime scene? Who was in charge of the investigation? Barney Fife? I have never heard of such careless regard for the public. In Dallas, that would *never* have happened, I can assure you."

Gustav answered, "None of the other guests, including your mother, was ever at risk as it was a targeted occurrence committed by a very sad young woman who is currently in the Jeffersonville jail. Detective Chestnut was in charge of the investigation and I am certain that she can allay any of your fears towards these events in regards to your mother. Again, I have absolutely no idea where she is. Does she live in Dallas?"

Charles replied, "No, she lives in Oklahoma City. That was going to be quite a long drive for her and we had convinced her to stay overnight in Dallas but, as I have stated, she never arrived."

Gustav asked, "Have you checked with her neighbors in Oklahoma? Maybe she decided to go straight home or maybe her phone battery died. She may be resting today, waiting to hear from you, not realizing her phone is dead. It happens, you know."

Charles countered, "Of course we have checked with the neighbors. No one has seen her and her car is not there. My mother is very responsible, and would let us know if she changed her plans like that."

Gustav replied, "Well, I do not have any more information for you. I wish you all the best in finding her quickly. Thank you for calling."

Then, he hung up the phone, and went to find Olive and Jackson. He called them both into the office, and told them of the disturbing call, and that his next call would be to Detective Chestnut. He had a very bad feeling about this, but tried to stay as positive as he could with Olive and Jackson.

Olive, of course, went to pieces. "I *knew* something bad was going to come of this with that woman! You don't think she has been *murdered* do you? Maybe there was more than one murderer in our inn!"

Gustav replied, "Please, calm down. *No*, I am sure she has not been murdered. The only murder that happened here was sad and the person is currently in the jail under lock and key. No need to worry. You saw how grateful the others were when they left here? Some of them have already written wonderful reviews. They are not murderers."

This helped to calm Olive and she and Jackson went on about their duties. Gustav immediately called the detective to let her know of Charles Castleberry's call, and gave her a heads up for when he, undoubtedly, would be calling her.

Detective Chestnut then informed Gustav about the arraignment, and the upcoming trial in January. Gustav immediately started worrying about all the publicity that surely would follow. So, he needed to implement his plan of the caroling and cookies event quickly to build as much good will as possible.

Chapter 37
Renata's Disappearance

Detective Sara Chestnut had a lot on her plate that day with the arraignment surprise and the impending trial. She knew that every detail of the investigation would be put under a microscope by the defense team for Scarlett Johnson. Then, on top of all of that, the call from Gustav, The Mistletoe Inn owner, to warn her of another potentially explosive situation regarding that investigation. When the phone rang, she was somewhat prepared for Charles Castleberry.

Charles started out, "What kind of investigation did you run that allowed a murderer to still stay in that inn with the other guests? You should have simply declared the inn as a crime scene, and investigated properly."

Detective Chestnut replied, "Sir, I am sorry you do not agree with my method of investigation into this situation but I can assure you that *no* other guest was ever in danger. The accused simply targeted the one guest that she felt had ruined her life. No other guests were ever involved. Now, she is in our jail, and facing a trial on January 15th for murder."

Charles continued, "Well, if no other guest was ever in danger, where is my mother and why did she not come to Dallas when she was supposed to do last night?"

Detective Chestnut answered, "I have no idea where your mother might be. Could she have changed her mind, and gone to visit a friend close by?"

Charles then informed the detective of the frantic phone messages he and his brother received, and her wording, which left them questioning everything that had happened at The Mistletoe Inn during her stay.

The detective was surprised, but chose to stay professional as she simply stated that the missing persons report states that a person must be missing for at least 48 hours for the police to investigate. She tried to calm him down by other suggestions of possibilities that he might not have considered. However, at the back of her mind, she had a suspicion that all was not well and that this investigation could soon take another turn. She promised Charles her full cooperation in searching for his mother, and proceeded to ask her assistant, Gary, to check the local hospitals within a 100-mile radius for Renata in case there had been an accident.

Sara was apprehensive about dealing with Charles as she remembered how hostile Renata had been regarding the information about her husband being in prison for embezzlement. Perhaps she needed to place another call to that Oklahoma lawyer, Jeff Willingham, to let him know all of this, and to give him a heads up about her being missing.

Chapter 38
Renata's Case

Attorney Jeff Willingham was just about to go home from Live Well Pharmaceuticals when his phone rang. He saw that it was Detective Chestnut again. "Hello Detective. What may I help you with?" Jeff answered.

"Well, this is a call to give you a heads up on a potentially bad situation coming your way. I just got off the phone with Charles Castleberry, the son of Renata Castleberry. It seems they can not find her. She did not arrive in Dallas, as was planned, to meet her sons, nor did she drive home to Oklahoma City. Her phone is off and he is panicking after hearing of the events from last week. He called The Mistletoe Inn, spoke with the owner, and then called me, extremely unhappy that his mother was allowed to stay in the inn after a murder had taken place. Gustav and I tried to tell him that no other guest was ever in any danger but he is simply not having it. I did not tell him about the other guests but he probably will contact you to find out all the details because his mother had left him a voicemail that stated they have a new case now to sue Live Well Pharmaceuticals due to all these wrongs that occurred. I sincerely hope that the embezzlement case was handled properly...all the i's dotted, and the t's crossed."

Jeff responded, "I am going over the records with a fine-toothed comb, I can assure you. As I recall, it was open and shut as he was caught red handed. The wife just simply refused to believe her husband would do such a thing. But, thank you for the heads up. I will certainly check into this on my own with everyone here who played a part in the original investigation. I also will drive by, and check on her home here in Oklahoma City, her neighbors,

Mistletoe, Murder, and Mayhem

etc." Jeff hung up the phone, and called his wife to tell her he would be late once again. He then looked up Renata's address, and set his GPS to drive there.

Jeff arrived at the house, parked across the street, and started checking around the front, side, and, from what he could see, the back of the house. No sign of her there. He then went to the next door neighbors, and asked if they had seen her, stating that her sons were concerned. No one had seen or heard from her but he handed them his card, and asked them to please call him when she came home. He told them it was purely a wellness check, explained where he worked, and again mentioned her son, Charles. Hopefully, Renata would arrive that night and there would be a logical explanation for all of this.

Jeff started for home, and tried to think of anything else that could have happened. She seemed unbalanced at their last meeting but *surely* she would not do anything crazy, like go off the grid to plan something sinister...would she? This put their original case against her husband on the forefront of Jeff's to-do list. He truly *must* go over every detail, and speak to everyone who played a part in this, just to be sure there was no wrongdoing...

Chapter 39:
Tuesday

Gustav went to the chamber of commerce meeting with flyers in hand to promote the caroling and cookies event. Jackson had done a great job on the flyer and the members seemed excited. Yes, some had questions about rumors they had heard about the murder but he addressed them succinctly, and was all smiles. Next, he went downtown to the historic square, visited with the shop owners, and distributed flyers there as well. The event was scheduled for the following Tuesday evening. Some immediately put the flyers on their front doors so that shoppers could see them as well.

He then went to the police department, and dropped off flyers for Detective Chestnut and her assistant, Gary. They were both quite busy but he was sure they would be interested in participating.

He was quite happy with himself when he arrived at the inn, sure that his idea would work in many ways. Olive was feeling better since there was no more bad news that day and she was excited about the event. She had been working on her Christmas trivia all morning, and could not wait to show it to Gustav, with Jackson waiting to do flyers for the guests.

Jackson had been busy on the phone as well, securing a fun band for Saturday night's ugly sweater contest. The guests could dance and sing along as this band played all the favorites. He was quite proud of this idea and could not wait to share it with Gustav and Olive.

They decided to have lunch together at a local diner to celebrate all the good news. Cyndy's Diner was a popular spot for locals, serving good food at reasonable prices, and the servers all chatted with the locals. They were seated in a booth so Olive and Jackson had plenty of room to show the others their work. They were in the middle of enjoying their lunches, and hearing all of that, when they were interrupted by a reporter for the Tyler newspaper who was asking all of them about the murder. Gustav handled it well as Olive and Jackson sat quietly observing. Gustav ended his answers to the reporter by announcing the caroling and cookies event, which was sure to be a local favorite. This turned the negative press around and, hopefully, people would not dwell on the crime but, instead, on the upcoming Christmas event.

Jackson was amazed, and very proud of the way his dad handled the situation. Cyndy, the owner of the diner, apologized for the reporter's rude interruption, and promised to hang one of the caroling and cookies event flyers on her front door. The patrons at the diner seemed quite pleased when the reporter left and they had nothing but good things to say about Gustav and Olive, who had immersed themselves in the community, and were good partners with the merchants.

When they arrived back at the inn, they put the new plans into motion. Jackson was busy making flyers for the Christmas trivia, and booking the band that he had secured. Olive was putting together the itinerary for the guests arriving on Thursday, and Gustav busied himself with collecting prizes for Christmas trivia, music bingo, and the ugly sweater contest. He visited the downtown merchants again to purchase the gifts, further showing goodwill to the town that had accepted them so well.

Detective Chestnut and Gary were busy on Tuesday calling every hospital, and exhausting every idea of where that missing woman might be. They certainly did not want any more trouble from her family. Also, the detective had looked into the public records from the embezzlement trial to see if she could find anything that could *possibly* be misconstrued as unfair. It looked completely legit to her as he was literally caught red handed with the cash in his bank account showing the transfer he had made that very day from the Live Well accounts. She also researched him, and saw that he had never had so much as a speeding ticket. What would make him act so out of character? Hopefully, Jeff Willingham would be able to figure all that out before it all blew up again.

Jeff Willingham had one thing on his mind as he entered Live Well Pharmaceuticals on Tuesday. He was going to speak with every person who worked with, or had any involvement with, the Castleberry embezzlement case. He called each person one at a time and had them come into the office (formerly Mr. Fathom's office) to ask them to remember all they could about the case and the arrest. It seemed they were tipped off by a new accounting hire who was charged with reconciling the bank statements, and then watched him secretly until they, indeed, caught him in the act of making a transfer into his account. The police were called and he was arrested. He did not say much in his statement, and pled guilty, but apparently told his wife he felt he was owed this money due to being promised bonuses that were never paid. Unfortunately, none of those promises were in writing so it was his word against Mr. Fathom's and he was proven guilty, and was subsequently given a ten year prison sentence.

There were records of his wife calling and harassing Mr. Fathom but nothing to warrant calling the police. She was labeled hysterical, and, eventually, the calls stopped. Ben Fathom had felt sorry for her, and felt that, since she was not at fault, she should have received one of the settlements. That gave him an idea. Did she cash or deposit the settlement? He would keep an eye on the bank records to check. That would give an important clue as to her whereabouts. He made a note to tell the detective that information if she called again. It was a sizable amount so, if there was foul play, someone would certainly cash it somewhere.

Jeff left for home, and stopped by a local florist to pick up a bouquet to smooth things over at home. Hopefully, they could spend a quiet evening at home focusing on their family rather than his work.

Chapter 40:
The Search Begins

Charles Castleberry and his brother, Michael, had been in contact with every family friend known to them to try and figure out where Renata might have gone. They had decided Charles would go to Renata's house in the hopes there would be some sort of clue. It had now been forty-eight hours since either of them had heard from her and the only clue she had left them was that she had mentioned suing the pharmaceutical company that had prosecuted their dad for embezzlement two years prior. What new information could she have found out? They had caught him in the act of transferring money into his account from the company. Renata just would not accept that, and blamed the company and its lawyer for putting her husband in prison, and thereby ruining her life. Charles agreed to go to visit that company to see what he could find out for himself.

Michael was calling hospitals from Jeffersonville to Dallas to see if she had been admitted, or worse. Maybe whatever she learned at that inn pushed her over the edge. She certainly sounded unstable on those messages. Surely, she did not do anything crazy. Suddenly, he felt guilty for not taking her calls at times, and not visiting. She was just crazed when she talked about missing their old life, and not moving on with her new reality. She had stopped seeing most of her friends, and going out at all, for the most part.

That is why it was so curious that she suddenly went on that weekend trip. She claimed it was a gift from their dad. How could that be? Michael admitted he had not visited, nor spoken to his dad in prison. He nor Charles had any desire to see him. They felt he had really let them all down, especially Renata. Now, in

Dallas, they were not around all the gossip about their family. Dallas is a big city and people are from everywhere. You can tell only what *you* decide to friends and acquaintances. But, they did feel sorry for Renata who just could not seem to move on. Now what? Maybe, while Charles went to Oklahoma City, he would go to Jeffersonville, and see what he could find out there. Hmm...that is an idea. He popped open a beer, and started planning his trip. He would leave the following day, and check out that inn, and see what he could find out.

Chapter 41:
Wednesday in Jeffersonville

Wednesday dawned on a cold December day in Jeffersonville. People were out Christmas shopping, looking for those last-minute gifts as the holiday was fast approaching. There were less than two weeks left and holiday events were happening everywhere. Christmas music was being played in every store and restaurant and, in general, spirits were high. Detective Sara Chestnut was one of those who needed a couple of gifts for her young niece and nephew, who she was certainly looking forward to seeing soon. She always felt it magical to see Christmas through the eyes of a child. Even with her job, which sometimes showed her the worst of humanity, she always loved Christmas, and felt so moved by the love of her fellow man towards her and her colleagues. She was looking forward to the caroling and cookies event at The Mistletoe Inn the following week. Perhaps she would see it in a different light, other than that of a crime scene. Her assistant, Gary, was also looking forward to it and she suspected that it was for more than one reason. He seemed really taken by that maid, Bambi Lynn, and she with him. Hmmm...maybe they would share a kiss under the mistletoe. *No mistletoe.* She would never see that plant in the same again. No romance there. It was just an evil poison, waiting for some desperate person to use it for killing someone else.

While she was out shopping, she stopped in at Cyndy's Diner for a quick bite, and caught Cyndy's eye as she was seated. Cyndy came over, and quietly told her about the reporter from Tyler who had been there the previous day. She had hoped everything would all die down now that the girl had been arraigned, and was awaiting trial. Detective Chestnut was not surprised, but managed to keep a straight face, and thanked her for the information. She needed to call on Gustav, and make sure he was okay. She did feel sorry for the owners as they had done nothing to deserve this and she knew they had been struggling. Maybe the upcoming event would help with positive publicity for the inn.

As she was leaving the diner, a young man stopped her, and asked if he could speak with her.

She said, "Do I know you?"

He replied, "I am Michael Castleberry and I am here searching for my mother, Renata Castleberry. Apparently, she was last seen leaving the parking lot of some inn here, and has not been seen or heard from since. Can you help me?"

Detective Chestnut answered, "I spoke with your brother yesterday, and told him everything I know about locating a missing person. I saw her at the inn twice and she checked out on Sunday. That is the last anyone I know has seen her in Jeffersonville."

Michael asked, "Would you please put out a missing person's report here since this is the last place she was known to be?"

Detective Chestnut answered, "I can. However, normally those reports are made where the person lives. Where does she live?"

Michael answered, "Oklahoma City but she never made it there."

Detective Chestnut asked, "Do you know that for sure?"

Michael responded, "Well, not exactly but we have been everywhere we can think she could have gone but no one has seen her. I have checked every hospital from here to Dallas where she had made plans to meet my brother and I on Sunday evening. Nothing. I guess that is good in a way but that means she has just disappeared."

Detective Chestnut agreed, and asked Michael to follow her back to the police station where she had Gary take down all the information needed for a missing person's report. Since Renata was technically a senior citizen at sixty, a silver alert could be issued. Michael gave Gary the make and model of her car, and the license plate number

Then, it was on to The Mistletoe Inn to introduce him to Gustav, and, hopefully, he would see that nothing had happened there. She gave Gustav a quick call to tell him they were on their way so he would be ready for them.

When Gary had finished with the reports needed, Detective Chestnut gave Michael a ride to The Mistletoe Inn.

Chapter 42:
Questions and More Questions

As they approached the inn, Michael was looking at the scenery, trying to get a feel for this small East Texas town. At the inn, they were greeted by Jackson, and then Gustav and Olive together. Jackson went into the kitchen, and had Chef Marta brew some tea, and make some coffee to warm them up. Soon, she brought out a tray with coffee, tea, and homemade cookies.

Michael began, "So, my mother left my brother and I some frantic voice messages on Sunday about learning some new information about the company that my dad used to work at, the one that he stole money from. Do you know what she was referring to? She said she had information that would enable us to sue the company and all would be well. She said she had learned some information during her stay here and that, now, she was certain that a lawyer would take our case. She made plans to see us on Sunday evening in Dallas but she never arrived at either my brother's place, or mine, nor at her home in Oklahoma City. This is incredibly strange and out of character, even for her."

Gustav said, "I am so very sorry about this and I wish I could tell you what she meant but what I can tell you is that she was very angry when she left here on Sunday. At breakfast, Jeff Willingham, Mr. Fathom's lawyer, came, and addressed the guests. He said that, since Mr. Fathom of the pharmaceutical company was deceased, and had no heirs, he had been given instructions by the elder Mr. Fathom, who had also recently passed, to give some settlement funds to the guests they had invited here. They felt Mr. Fathom had wronged them in one way or another. All of the guests came up, received their envelopes, and thanked him, except for your mother. She was incredibly angry, and told him no amount of money could bring back her life, which she claimed he had ruined. Then, she stomped off to her room. A while later, when she came to check out, we simply thanked her, and told her, just like the other guests, that we hoped she would consider staying here again. She was furious and said *no* because there were too many bad memories here. Then, she said that we had not heard the last of her, and walked out. We have no idea what she meant but those were the last words she spoke here."

Michael was almost apologetic as he said, "Yes, she sounded just like that on my voice message and then she just seemed to disappear. So, you say she had an envelope with money in it?"

Gustav said, "Whether it was cash or a check, we do not know. We simply saw him hand them out to the guests."

Detective Chestnut intervened, "Hmmmm…now there could be a motive for foul play. Maybe she stopped for gas and a stranger accosted her. We have put out a silver alert for her and, hopefully, someone will have seen something."

Gustav asked, "Michael, are you planning on staying a while in Jeffersonville?"

Michael spoke, "Yes, I checked into the Marriott when I arrived. I did not know how long I would need to be here so I just found a place on the freeway."

At that, Detective Chestnut said, "Well, if that is all, I really need to be getting back to the station."

They said their goodbyes and Michael got back into her car. She drove him to the station, and promised to update him with any information.

She had a very bad feeling about this situation, but tried to not let it show to Michael as she shook his hand, nor to Gary at the station.

Chapter 43:
Wednesday in Oklahoma City

Jeff arrived at Live Well Pharmaceutical's office with the agenda of checking on the progress on finding candidates for the CEO position. He had just settled in when the receptionist called to tell him he had a visitor. He went to greet the visitor who turned out to be Charles Castleberry, the son of the man in prison. Jeff shook his hand, and invited him into his office. He spoke first, "What may I do to help you?"

Charles answered, "My mother called me and my brother on Sunday afternoon, frantic, and made plans to meet us in Dallas that evening to discuss what all she had learned at that inn. She said she was certain that a lawyer would take our case. Then, she just seemingly disappeared. No more phone calls or texts, no meetings, no nothing. What on Earth happened there? What did she mean by all that she had learned? She was talking about suing this company. I just need some answers because this is starting to sound like something on Nightline."

Jeff answered, "I am not totally sure of what she meant in that message. You do know that Mr. Fathom was murdered there, and every guest was questioned, but the new information to help your family sue? No clue what she meant. I went there on Sunday morning to apologize to each guest because I was the one who had invited them to the inn. You see, my employer, Mr. Ben Fathom, Nigel Fathom's uncle, had been keeping tabs on his nephew for some time, and knew of circumstances where Mr. Fathom had wronged people. He had me invite them there for Mr. Fathom to make amends as I had seriously instructed him to do. But, then, he was murdered hours after he arrived. Yes, by one of the guests. That person did not work here but he had taken her parents from her as a child by a drunk driving accident and he had, with my assistance, gotten off with a slap on the wrist. Now, in your mother's case, Ben Fathom felt she deserved some funds to help her because your dad's retirement was forfeited after he stole from the company. I did hand her the envelope with a generous amount of money in it but she flew into a rage, and told me no amount of money could make up for what we took from her. That was the last I saw of her. Now, I took it upon myself to check into every detail of your dad's case yesterday. I cannot find *any* abnormality whatsoever. I do not know what she can be so angry at us for."

Charles took all this in, and simply said "Thank you for your time." He could not get out of there fast enough. The last thing he needed was another reminder of what his dad had put their family through. Now, to go to her house. As he drove to her neighborhood, he nervously thought about the what ifs in this situation. What if she had gone off the deep end, and just decided to start over with the money he had given her? Then, why leave those messages for he and Michael? No, that was not it.

He pulled into the driveway, used the spare key hidden in a plant, and entered the empty house. No one appeared to have been here for several days. The plants were wilting for lack of water and the mail was stacked up in the mailbox. Where was Renata? He decided to go to both neighbors' houses, and ask them. No one had seen nor heard from her since the previous week. Just then, his phone rang. It was Michael.

Michael told Charles all that he had learned. Then, it was Charles' turn to inform Michael about his visit with the lawyer. They were more confused and concerned by the minute. Charles decided to stay the night in the house, just I case, and they agreed to speak again the following day.

After looking in the refrigerator, Charles decided to go out, and have dinner. Hopefully, that would take his mind off the increasingly strange situation. He settled on a quiet place near downtown, and ordered a beer.

Chapter 44:
Thursday in Jeffersonville

Thursday morning dawned with the sun shining brightly. Gustav felt that was a sign of good things with the new guests scheduled to arrive that day. He was in a good mood, bustling around, and checking every detail.

Jackson had the itinerary for each guest for the special events planned, starting that night with ornament making.

Bambi Lynn was in charge of that night's festivities, with Chef Marta making cookies and hot chocolate. Hopefully, the new round of guests would not have a murderer among them, thought Bambi Lynn. She was planning to find out as much as she could about each one that night just in case. A girl could not be too careful.

Just then, all their cell phones went off with an alert. It was a silver alert about their former guest, Renata Castleberry. *Wow!* Now they had a missing person's case as well as a murder. Bambi Lynn began to think she was not as safe as she had been led to believe. However, that woman has been clearly unbalanced. Anyone could see that with her yelling at everyone.

Michael awoke in his hotel room with the sun streaming in the windows. He showered, dressed quickly, and then checked his phone as he waited for his coffee to brew. There was nothing new so he decided to go down to breakfast, and had just gotten seated when his phone went off with the silver alert for his mother. That should work! Surely, someone will have seen something. He would call Charles when he finished breakfast because he probably would not have seen it.

When he and Charles had spoken the previous night, and compared notes, they both had learned of the envelope of money given to Renata just before she left. That as an interesting fact. Surely, it could be traced if it was a check, and was cashed. Maybe it was cash. Then, there would be no trace unless it was deposited into her bank account. That is it! He had access as a signer on her account. He would call the bank, and ask if there had been any deposits or, for that matter, hits on her credit card. That, too, would be a clue. Now, he had a plan.

Chapter 45:
Thursday in Oklahoma City

Charles woke up in Renata's house to a cold, dreary December day. Just a few days left till Christmas and all he could think about was the mess. Coffee…he needed coffee. Where did she keep it? Okay, found it. He would get Starbucks later. This would do for now to give him some clarity. He got into the shower, got dressed, and was just about to make a plan for the day when his phone rang. It was Michael. Michael told him he had called the bank and there had been no deposits, nor any credit card activity since the previous Saturday in downtown Jeffersonville. Well, that was telling. Where could she be where she did not need any funds? Michael also told him about the silver alert. That was progress. He was so thankful they had done that. It seemed like Michael was in the right place.

Charles made plans to join him the following Friday as he wanted one more day there to check out one more lead he had thought of. It was the lawyer they had hired to help them with his dad's trial. He had done an okay job; probably all that could be done since they basically had caught him in the act and he had pled guilty. He searched in the house until he found a document with the lawyer's name on it.

Now, he had a plan. As he was driving over to the law office, he planned what he was going to say. Hopefully, he could find out something that could help them find Renata.

When he arrived, the receptionist greeted him, and asked him if he had an appointment. He confessed he did not but he did say it was a matter of urgency. He just needed a few moments of the lawyer's time. She disappeared and, when she returned, she said that, yes, the lawyer would see him. She ushered him into the office and Charles greeted the lawyer, apologizing for just popping by, but explaining that it was a serious situation. He enlightened him on the missing person case, and asked if there was *any* reason he could think of that would explain why Renata just would *not* believe his dad was guilty?

The lawyer looked up their case and, after a few moments, answered, "No, not at all. She just would not believe it. I have notes here that your dad pled guilty. They basically found him transferring the money from the company to his account and, from there, it was just a paper trail of transfer after transfer. My job was just to get him the best plea deal possible. Your mother was furious with me, and felt I did not do my job."

Charles thanked him, and left more determined than ever to join his brother in Jeffersonville, and hopefully get some answers.

Chapter 46:
Scarlett's Defense

Attorney Robert Blake spent Tuesday and Wednesday going over every news article and public record, and interviewing Scarlett herself about the accident that killed her parents all those years ago. Her aunt and uncle, whom took her in, and raised her afterwards, provided some background as well. The conclusion was that it was a terrible accident where a drunk driver was not held accountable, but only given community service. How? Because his legal team was far superior to the local prosecutor.

Robert determined he definitely needed to speak to the lead attorney, Jeff Willingham, about this. When he saw the name, he wrote down a list of things to discuss with Mr. Willingham. They included: 1. Miscarriage of justice regarding this accident. 2. Monies given to the aunt and uncle from Jeff Willingham during the years for Scarlett's education. Blood money? 3. Why could he possibly think getting all these people together in one place with the man who, according to Scarlett, had wronged them all would end well? 4. Now what?

Also on Robert's to-do list was speaking to the inn owner about what exactly transpired. He would need statements from all involved: staff and the other guests.

Would any of this exonerate Scarlett? No, but it could show many reasons why she acted as she did, which could evoke sympathy for her, translating into a much more lenient sentence, unless he could prove that she did not act alone. According to her recounting of the Saturday night arrest, many secrets were revealed and each guest had a strong motive for wanting justice from the deceased. There was no escaping her confession because she made it in front of a group of witnesses but maybe duress or her state of mind would be brought into question?

His next step was to contact Attorney Jeff Willingham, and get some answers.

Chapter 47:
Jeff Willingham Under Fire

Thursday dawned dreary and cold but it was mid-December in Oklahoma City so that was to be expected. After the previous day's meeting with Charles Castleberry, he felt relatively sure that the missing woman was no more of his concern. He had much bigger issues to tackle anyway. He felt sorry for the sons, but felt it was no more of his concern. He needed to move on with the company choosing the new leadership. The board was slowly sending him candidates to vet for the position and he was liking what he was seeing. It would be his job to see if any of the Live Well Pharmaceutical employees were candidates as it would be a wonderful start to the new year if a promoted, dedicated employee could lead them. He was not sure yet if any of them were suitable, so that day, he was looking at their employee files.

Just then, the receptionist buzzed him to say a Robert Blake was on the phone for him. He had no idea who that was so he trepidatiously picked up the phone, and said "Hello, this is Jeff Willingham. How may I help you?"

Robert started off, "This is attorney Robert Blake. My client Scarlett Johnson has given me your name in relation to our case. Do you have some time to talk this morning?"

Jeff answered "Yes, I do. Once again, what can I help you with? I was not present at the inn when the murder occurred..."

Robert interrupted, "Well, that is just one thing I want to discuss with you. Apparently, *you* invited all those guests to an inn, fully knowing their history with the deceased, and I am absolutely clueless about what you were thinking, and what you hoped to achieve."

Jeff answered, "Correction. My employer, Ben Fathom, uncle of the deceased, had me invite them all. I did caution him about the potential volatile situations that could erupt but he insisted. You see, I had a talk with the younger Mr. Fathom ninety days before that, showing him the files on the guests, and begging him to make things right with them, whatever it took. Ben was adamant that his nephew complete this task but, after two months had passed, he had not even made contact with any of them. So, we went to Plan B, which we had already set into motion by sending out those invitations to the five people, offering them a free four-night stay at the quaint inn, with holiday-themed experiences for them."

Robert said, "Okay, now that makes a bit more sense to me, except why was his uncle so insistent that he do the right thing for those five people?"

Jeff answered immediately, "Because, many years before that, Ben had been a hard man, ruthless to some, and alone when, one Christmas, he experienced a total spiritual revival and, from then on, he was a wonderful boss, and a friend to many, sharing his wealth with many individuals. Over the years, he had been watching his nephew closely, and determined he was following the exact same path as him. He had tried many times to talk with him, and mentor him to change, but all to no avail. So, he decided to appeal to the only thing that seemed to matter to him, *money*. When I met with the nephew, I informed him that him not making amends with those people would severely affect his inheritance, and to take the matter seriously. But, just in case, we set him up with a reservation at the inn as well, to reward him for his good deeds, or so we told him. Then, as time progressed, we stressed he *must* go to that weekend of Christmas-themed activities because his uncle demanded it. I am quite certain that was the only reason he was there."

Robert answered, "Well, that is quite the story. Ok, now to talk about the guests involved. Let's start with my client, Scarlett Johnson. I have been researching the accident and, for the life of me, I cannot possibly understand why Fathom was not convicted of intoxication manslaughter. Can you enlighten me?"

Jeff sighed, and answered "That was because it was a downpour rain event that night, their car seemingly had veered into the other lane, and, with low visibility, coupled with impaired reactions, Mr. Fathom hit them head on, killing both of them instantly. He was immediately taken to the nearest hospital and I was called to be with him, handling the police investigation. His blood did register above the legal limit but extenuating circumstances, plus his clean record, and the offer to pay regular payments for their child's education and upbringing, which we did, got him community service, a slap on the wrist."

Robert answered, "Do you think justice was served for my client?"

Jeff answered, "No jail or prison time would bring back her parents so, in a way, yes. Although, she certainly did not think so, apparently."

Robert asked, "Would you?"

Jeff answered, "Hard to say. Grief is a terrible thing; different for everyone."

Robert thanked Jeff for his time, and ended the call. He had documented all that Jeff had told him, and needed time to process it.

Jeff, after the call, just *Do Not Disturb* on his phone, and put his head in his hands. Was Mr. Blake right? Did he facilitate the murder, inadvertently of course? Now that there would be a jury trial, this would be yet another nightmare that he needed to survive. First things first: Reviewing the file on the accident, going over every detail, witness statement, etc. Secondly, he would have to tell the board everything about the case, and to be prepared for a legal battle.

Chapter 48:
Guests Arrive

Jackson was ready as the first guests appeared at the Inn. The first was a lovely couple, Carol and Harold Davis, who were there to enjoy an anniversary weekend full of Christmas activities. They were very excited to take part in all the fun and Jackson gave them the Victorian Christmas Room. They took their key, went to find their room, eagerly opened the door, and then started taking photos. They loved all the exquisite décor with a romantic feel, and quickly unpacked so they could start exploring before that night's ornament making. It would be the perfect 39th Anniversary trip.

The next guest was Charlene Moseby, an older woman who was definitely interested in the Christmas activities, and asked about nearby shopping. Jackson gave her the map to the historic downtown. Jackson gave her the Silver Bells Room and she was amazed by the beautiful décor. She decided to take a nap before exploring all the shops, and quickly went to sleep.

Next was a single gentleman, Cameron Mathis. He said he was intrigued by the holiday-themed stay, and was eager to participate in all the activities. Jackson handed him the key to the Silver and Gold Room upstairs. He headed up the stairs, and, happy with the room, quickly unpacked. Cameron was actually a travel writer who was there to review the inn. He had specifically asked for the Silver and Gold Room, very much aware of what had recently happened there. He wanted to experience all of it himself before he wrote the article. He had been asked to report on the death, and what led up to it, as well as what he experienced there. His company was very explicit on his instructions so they could determine exactly how to rate the inn and its reputation. That, presumably, could make or break The Mistletoe Inn. Cameron would happily participate, experience everything, ask for room service, and only then write the article. He had to keep his secret while he was there so as to not receive any special treatment, or careful exclusion.

Jason thought to himself, what a difference with those guests. No one seemed odd or difficult to him. Whew! Maybe this group would just be fun, which was exactly what the holiday-themed events were supposed to be.

Just when he thought he was done, two men approached, both with luggage. He asked them, "Welcome to The Mistletoe Inn. May I help you?"

One of them said, "Hello I am Charles Castleberry and I would like two rooms please, one for me and one for my brother, Michael, if you have availability. When I checked online, it appeared you did have rooms."

Jackson then knew exactly who they were, and said, "Yes, sir. We have two rooms available. Blue Christmas and The Cardinal Rooms are both available. Would you please sign in and I will need to secure a credit card for each."

Michael and Charles each presented their credit cards and Jackson gave them each keys, as well as the itinerary of holiday events, and the map to the historic downtown square for shopping. Charles looked at Michael, shrugged, and said, "Why not? We are here to research the area, look for our mother, and retrace her steps." They headed to their rooms and Jackson went in search of Gustav to report the latest development.

Chapter 49: Gustav

When Jackson found Gustav, he and Olive were going over all the details of the upcoming events. He relayed the message that they had two new guests: Charles and Michael Castleberry. That was quite a surprise for all of them but Gustav felt no alarm. After all, they had nothing to do with Renata's disappearance. He understood them retracing her steps. That made perfect sense to him. Just what they thought they could learn at the inn was the question.

Gustav told Jackson and Olive they would all make sure to go out of their way to show the two brothers a wonderful time. Maybe it would make them feel not quite so scared. After all, surely she would turn up soon. At least, that was his hope.

Around five that afternoon, another gentleman came to the front desk, and asked for Gustav. Jackson asked his name and he answered, "Robert Blake." Jackson went and found Gustav to inform him of Mr. Blake wanting to speak with him.

Gustav went to the lobby, and greeted Mr. Blake. He ushered him into the dining room, empty at that point. Gustav began, "What may I help you with, Mr. Blake?"

Blake responded, "I am the attorney for Miss Scarlett Johnson and I have several questions for you. I understand that your chef served the deceased Mr. Fathom a tray. Is that normal practice for you?"

Gustav answered, "No sir. We only serve breakfast and refreshments at our holiday events. Nothing else."

Mr. Blake continued, "Then, why did your chef serve Mr. Fathom a tray, and leave it outside his door? You do realize that *anyone* could have tampered with it without being seen. I understand you do not have security cameras, correct?"

Gustav answered, "No, we do not have cameras as we always felt that would be an invasion of privacy for our guests. Yes, that was an unfortunate error on our chef's part. The tray was covered with a dome, but, to your point, one of the guests could have had some access to it. Obviously, your client did. Now, why our chef took him food at all was her trying to accommodate a very difficult guest who refused to be a part of the activities, and kept on saying he was starving. She felt sorry for him. She was already in the kitchen preparing food, and felt it was not that much of an imposition to take him a turkey sandwich and a soda."

Robert Blake answered, "I see. Did anyone see my client leave the event, and tamper with the tray?"

Gustav answered, "I am not quite sure. You would have to question each of them, or ask Detective Chestnut."

Bambi Lynn and Chef Marta began to go in to set up for the ornament making event and Gustav rose, and said, "I am sorry but I must help my staff with preparations for this evening's activity. I hope I have answered all of your questions sufficiently."

Robert simply said, "Thank you. That is all for now. I will reserve the right to come again if I have any more questions." With that, he left the inn, and headed back to his office to go over all he had learned that day.

Gustav called the staff together in the kitchen, and informed them of the visit. Chef Marta was again worried until Gustav told her what he had said to the attorney. Gustav told them, "Come and find me if he reappears. Do not speak with him without me present. Understood?" They all agreed. Gustav added, "Great. Now, let's give our guests a wonderful evening of ornament making and treats, shall we? No more talk of murder or poison."

Chapter 50:
The Search Begins

Charles and Michael Castleberry awoke early on Friday, met in the dining room for breakfast, and discussed their agenda for the day. They were resolute in their plans to thoroughly search the area for any clues as to the whereabouts of Renata. They agreed their accommodations were fine, the breakfast was wonderful, and the other guests all seemed to be having a great time.

The previous night, they had gone to the ornament making event, and met the other guests, as well as got a feel for the staff. So far, no red flags were there.

The plan for that day was to retrace any route their mother could possibly have driven, and see if they could find any clue as to her whereabouts. They started out from the parking lot, and took the most obvious route at first, driving fifty miles away before circling back, and trying another route. They then drove in the town and around the nearby outskirts. Nothing they could see or even begin to guess was where she had been.

Famished, they stopped at Cyndy's Diner for some food. Detective Chestnut happened to be there and Michael introduced Charles to her and her assistant, Gary. They compared notes, and told her where they had looked, asking for more ideas. She said no leads had come in following the silver alert, which is very unusual. Normally, there would be many sightings, most of which would turn out to be false, But, at least there was something to investigate.

Charles asked her a difficult question, "Has this ever happened here before?"

Detective Chestnut answered, "Not since I have been here. I will check with my predecessor. Maybe he will know of a possibility that I do not." She asked them where they were staying, and was surprised to learn they were staying at The Mistletoe Inn.

Michael explained, "We felt it was important to get a real feel for what she experienced and maybe we would get a read on where she might have gone. We are still unable to reach her by phone."

Detective Chestnut answered, "Well, there is one thing. There has been no ransom demand so, more than likely, she was not kidnapped or you probably would have heard by now."

With that, she and her assistant left the diner and Charles and Michael discussed the conversation. It was not much consolation but it was something. They decided to have some MISSING posters made, and would put them up all over town, just in case someone had seen something.

They found a print shop, and ordered the posters to be picked up on Saturday.

By the time they arrived back at the inn, it was almost time for the Christmas trivia pizza night. They agreed to change, and meet in the lobby.

Chapter 51: Cameron's Quest

Cameron Mathis had been a reporter for Trips Around Texas magazine for several years. He had a great job traveling around the state, staying in bed and breakfasts, hotels, and inns, soaking up the local atmosphere, and then reporting back in the form of a full article. Occasionally, he would get sent out because of a news event, or, on rare occasions, a crime scene like this one. He was to fully experience the inn, the same room as the deceased man, and interact with the guests and the staff as much as possible. He decided to try the chef by calling down to the kitchen at three, and asking for a sandwich. He was told, in no uncertain terms, they did not provide room service. They recommended some local restaurants, and reminded him of pizza night, which would be later that evening.

That checked off the list, he had found nothing to complain about so far. The room was beautifully decorated and the gold and silver décor was stunning. The breakfast had been great that morning and the staff were very welcoming. The previous night, the ornament making was a great surprise. Each guest made two ornaments, which would make great gifts for friends or family.

His next step was to check out the downtown area and he left with the map. Nearby attractions were always a plus and that town had a historic square that many travelers love,. He was planning on taking many pictures that he could include in his article.

Chapter 52:
Christmas Trivia Night

At 7:00, all the guests were seated in the dining room, ready for pizza and a fun trivia night. Carol and Harold Davis had used the day to shop downtown, buying gifts for their family, and visited the local winery, toasting their anniversary.

Charlene Moseby had also been shopping for gifts, and had a lovely lunch at the Lavender Tea Room.

Cameron Mathis spent the afternoon exploring the historic sites downtown, and relaxed at the new brewery before coming back.

The brothers listened to all of this chatter and, when the attention was focused on them, they added exploring the area, and eating at Cyndy's Diner. They saw no reason to tell the other guests their real reason for being there. The staff did not divulge their ties to the former unpleasantness that the murder had brought. Then, the pizza was served and everyone was focused on eating and the Christmas trivia.

As the evening drew to a close, everyone was thrilled when the chef came out with an anniversary cake for Carol and Harold who were most grateful! Everyone joined in with a champagne toast to the couple.

As the guests all headed for their rooms, the clean-up began and the staff all remarked that it had gone very well indeed. Olive had done a superb job with the questions and the guests were very competitive. The prizes were great as well. Gustav had done an exceptional job there.

Sheila Williamson

But, the best part was the cake! Chef Marta had done an incredible job for the couple's anniversary. They appreciated it so much and all the guests enjoyed it.

Chapter 53:
Saturday

Saturday dawned on The Mistletoe Inn with clouds and much colder weather. The forecast was for possible snow flurries during the day, and getting heavier as the day wore on. The guests all made their way to breakfast, and were anxiously looking outside as all of them had activities planned. Gustav addressed their concerns, and offered the van to drive them anywhere they needed to go.

The Castleberry brothers were not concerned because they grew up in Oklahoma City, and had experienced much more snow than native Texans. Their only concern was the cold as they were planning to go door to door downtown with their MISSING flyers. The print shop was to have them ready by 10:00 so they were in the car and on their way by then.

Gustav had the van ready to drive Carol and Harold to their couple's massage they had booked in town, Charlene to the salon for a hair appointment, and Cameron to the museum for a scheduled tour.

All the guests were thrilled with this added service and it made for a lively ride. After he dropped them off, he headed to the police station to see if he could have a word with Detective Chestnut.

Gustav was in luck as the Detective and Gary were going over the information that the former detective had given her about any missing person's case before. He approached and she showed him into a conference room.

He spoke, "I just wanted you to know two things. One is that the brothers that are looking for their missing mother are staying with us now. I have told the staff to treat them extra carefully as they are obviously hurting. The other guests do not know anything about this. They have not shared and we certainly will not either. Secondly, I received a visit yesterday from Robert Blake, the attorney for Scarlett Johnson. It was quite the visit as he questioned me on everything. I refused to give him the contact information of the other guests, quoting privacy issues. It seems to me that he is going to try to have the confession thrown out, and is looking for another suspect. I assume this might be normal but, having never been involved in a murder case before, it's not to me."

Detective Chestnut looked at Gary, and then answered him, "I agree he is looking elsewhere trying to prove anything he can. I do not think it will work because all those witnesses heard Scarlett clearly confess. As to the brothers, yes, we ran into them at Cyndy's Diner yesterday. They are searching and searching every possible route from here for any sign of her. I can't say that I blame them. There has been no tip come through, nor any sighting of her since the silver alert went out. That is extremely odd, to say the least. Gary and I were just going over information from my predecessor. I called, and asked him if there had been an unsolved missing person's case while he was here. If so, what did they do that we have not in their search? He gave us some country road areas to check for ditches, etc."

Gustav took all this in, and answered, "Well, I will leave you to it. I need to get home to prepare for our ugly sweater contest night. You are both certainly welcome to join us if you like."

They looked at each other, and the detective said, "Well, that might not be the best idea, but let us discuss…"

Charles and Michael made their way downtown after picking up the posters, and started around the square, asking each merchant to please display them in the hopes that someone might come forward, and report seeing her, or her car at least. When they entered Cyndy's Diner, she was very happy to help, and even made an announcement to her packed restaurant. She asked for everyone's help in finding Renata. They both thanked her tremendously, and went on their way, ending at the Brewery that they had heard about the previous night from that guest. As they sipped their beers, they went over what they had learned. Then, they decided to visit the police station on their way back to The Mistletoe Inn.

When they walked in, they were ushered into the conference room where Gary, as well as Detective Chestnut, both joined them. They shared what all they had done and the detective shared what she had learned from her predecessor. They all decided on a plan to search on Sunday as the weather was supposed to break and the visibility would be better as the flurries were coming down right then.

When they had left, Detective Chestnut said, "I am rethinking this and it may be a good idea for us to attend tonight. Do you have an ugly Christmas sweater you can wear?"

Gary said while laughing, "Of course. My mom gives me one each year and I think they are all ugly."

So, they agreed to meet at The Mistletoe Inn at 7:00. There was nothing wrong with them having a little fun with the community. What could go wrong?

Chapter 54:
The Ugly Sweater Contest

At 7:00, the guests made their way to the dining room, laughing at each other's sweaters. It seemed the downtown merchants supplied all of them! It was amazing that all the designs were different!

The chef was bringing out Caesar salads, lasagna, and pasta primavera. The smells were mouthwatering. All the guests were sipping on glasses of wine to accompany the meal when two more guests arrived, Detective Chestnut and Gary, much to the delight of Bambi Lynn. Her eyes lit up when Gary entered the room.

Gustav introduced them to the guests since all but two would not have ever met them. He explained that he ran into them earlier, and thought it might be fun to incorporate them into the evening. The guests all applauded, and welcomed them.

When everyone had finished the delicious food, drinks were refreshed and then Jackson came up to introduce the entertainment. The band had gotten rave reviews downtown so he was very excited to have them at The Mistletoe Inn.

As they warmed up, the guests lined up, including Detective Chestnut and Gary. The band voted on the ugly sweater winners and Gary had been correct. His was the grand prize winner. Everyone clapped and then the band started playing.

Dessert was served and it seemed like everything was incredibly perfect...until a scream came from the kitchen!

Gustav and Detective Chestnut, as well as Gary, all ran toward the kitchen. When they arrived, they saw Chef Marta holding a huge knife and then they saw Bambi Lynn being choked by a man in a ski mask who kept warning Chef Marta to back up. The Spanish yelled between them seemed like they knew each other. Detective pushed her way in to the center, and pointed her firearm at the intruder, threatening him to let her go.

Gary was calling the station for back up while not taking his eyes off Bambi Lynn for a second. He would never forgive himself if anything happened to her. They had just started seeing each other but, already, they were getting very close.

Fortunately, Detective Chestnut was bilingual, and could interpret the conversation. It seemed this man knew Chef Marta's husband, and was threatening her about him. That part she could not quite make out. She spoke in Spanish to both of them, telling them to stop and that they needed to talk it out. No one needed to get hurt, but, if he kept choking her, *he* would get hurt. She would not be able to help him.

Then, in English, "Bambi Lynn, do you know this man?"

She replied "no" weakly because he was holding her so tightly around the neck.

"Well, then, I know you do not want to do this in front of two police officers and more are on the way," she spoke in Spanish to him.

Chef Marta was now crying, begging him to let her go in Spanish. "Chef Marta, who is this man?" asked the detective.

"He is my husband's cousin who is trying to get me to give him money *once again* or else he says he will have my husband killed."

By now, reinforcements had arrived through the back entrance. There were police surrounding them in the kitchen. There was no way out, as the detective pointed out. This would not end well if he did not let her go, and surrender himself. All of this was said in Spanish so he would understand. While she was talking to him, an officer came from behind, and grabbed him, loosening his grip on Bambi Lynn, who fell into Gary's arms.

The man was apprehended and Chef Marta was also taken in the car with Detective Chestnut so that they could work all of this out at the police station.

Everyone breathed a sigh of relief. No murder and no one seriously injured. Back to the guests who, thankfully, were unaware of this as they were listening to the band, and watching Carol and Harold dance. Even Michael asked Charlene to dance and so they were none the wiser. The band played for over an hour and Gustav was very relieved.

Gary stayed behind to make sure Bambi Lynn was okay, and to take her statement, asking if she needed to be checked out at the emergency room. She refused, and was happy for him to hold her, and be with her. He offered to drive her home. She accepted.

When the guests had all left the dining room, Gustav called Olive and Jackson into the kitchen to tell them what had happened earlier. They could not believe it! Olive was beside herself but Gustav focused them on cleaning up since Bambi Lynn was shaken up and Chef Marta was at the police station. They made a plan for making the Sunday breakfast, which was always a brunch, if she did not return. All the ingredients were in the refrigerator and pantry. They simply had to cook and serve the guests themselves.

The clean-up went well as everyone was quietly working, thinking about what might have been, and about the following morning. When alone, Olive went to pieces and Gustav had to hold her, comforting her to calm her to sleep.

Chapter 55:
Police Station

The station was all abuzz when the Detective, Chef Marta, and the officers, bringing the intruder in, all arrived. They went into interview rooms with the intruder being handcuffed and placed in one with an officer, and Chef Marta with the detective who immediately asked, "Now, let's start at the beginning. This man...how did he come to be in your kitchen tonight and, again, for the record, how do you know him?"

Chef Marta answered, "He came to the back door, and begged to be let in. We had words and I said no more money for him. This man is not a good man. He works for bad people in Mexico. I have helped him before since he was my husband's cousin, but no more. When I told him no, I grabbed the knife, and told him to get out. That is when he grabbed Bambi Lynn. I could not help it. I screamed. I was worried he would really hurt her."

Detective Chestnut continued, "How does he control what happens to your husband?"

Chef Marta answered, "My husband was deported back to Mexico over something that happened years ago and he does see him. My husband will not have anything to do with him and I have not told him I had given him money before."

She started sobbing so Detective Chestnut got her some tissues, and said, "Okay, tell me everything from before and then I can see what we can do."

Chef Marta told her the whole story of working at the senior living community and what happened there. She also told her that Gustav and Olive did not know anything about this because they did not really check her references once she first cooked for them. She had been so happy there and she told the detective about supporting her family, including her mother.

At that, the detective asked the cousin's name. Chef Marta replied, "Alejandro." Then, the detective left the room to go speak to Alejandro.

She asked for the interpreter on the force, Sgt. Garcia, to join them. They entered the room, released the officer watching him, and addressed Alejandro. The interpreter relayed the detective's questions in Spanish. What he was doing at the inn? Did he have a reason to be there and what did he hope to achieve by showing up?

He answered in Spanish that he was just visiting his cousin to give her a message from her husband in Mexico.

The told the interpreter to ask what the message was.

Alejandro answered that he needed money and that Marta needed to give it to him to help her husband.

They asked him if he worked for his cousin.

He answers not right then and that is why he needed the money.

They then asked why would Marta's husband not send his wife the message? Why would he send Alejandro, who she has given money to before?

He answered that his cousin was in some trouble, and needed the money to get out of it.

They asked him what kind of trouble he was in.

He answered that he doublecrossed some bad people.

Then, they asked, "The people *you* work for?"

He did not answer, but asked for a lawyer.

At that point, the detective left Sgt. Garcia there, and went back to Chef Marta to tell her what he said. Chef Marta assured her that Alejandro was lying, that the person in trouble was him, and that she would not help him.

Detective Chestnut believed her and decided to let her go, but told her she will be checking out all that Chef Marta said for accuracy. If she found out Marta was lying, she would immediately be arrested. Chef Marta agreed, and was driven back to the inn by a deputy.

Chapter 56:
Sunday

Sunday morning brunch went as scheduled at The Mistletoe Inn with Chef Marta back at the helm, as well as Bambi Lynn. All the guests enjoyed a fabulous breakfast of french toast, scrambled eggs, sausages, bacon, and fresh fruit parfaits. Pitchers of mimosas and coffee were served as well to very appreciative diners.

Gustav and Olive prepared for their guests to depart and Jackson was told he could take the afternoon off to be with friends. Chef Marta and Bambi Lynn were cleaning up the dining room and kitchen, nervously awaiting Gustav and Olive's questions that were sure to come.

The anniversary couple, Carol and Harold, were the first to leave and they promised a stellar review to Gustav after thanking him and Olive for a fabulous getaway!

Next was Cameron Mathis, who also was quite appreciative of the guest experience. He also promised a wonderful review.

The last of the original guests was Charlene Moseby, who gave Gustav and Olive a beautiful card that she had purchased downtown. She was so happy with her stay, and also promised a stellar review.

Next came Charles and Michael Castleberry. They had decided to head back to Dallas after chasing every lead they could imagine. Both were still hopeful that Renata would be found, but needed to get back to their lives until that time. They thanked both Gustav and Olive for treating them so well and said they both enjoyed their stay. They just wished it was for a different reason. Gustav and Olive hugged the men, and promised to keep in touch with any bit of news that would surface.

As they left the inn, it had just started to snow big powdery flakes and it somehow just fit the scenario.

Soon, the inn was empty of guests and Gustav and Olive headed to the kitchen to check with Chef Marta and Bambi Lynn. They found them sitting, having coffee and toast at the kitchen table, waiting to face their questions.

Gustav said, "Well, Chef, would you care to enlighten us on what happened last night? Who was that man? How did he get in? Why was he so angry? And, is he safely locked up?"

Chef Marta told them the entire story, starting with the senior living community, and then ending with the previous night's scary scenario. She assured them both that her cousin-in-law was indeed behind bars, and most likely would be deported back to Mexico unless they had enough to hold him here. She apologized for not totally telling them everything that had happened at her past job but they chose not to check deeply into her references. She had been so happy here that she almost forgot about the past troubles. But, lately, with the murder, and then last night, here they were. She begged them to let her stay, but told them she would understand if they thought she was a liability.

Bambi Lynn had been quiet until then, but decided to speak up, "Please do not let Chef go. She is such a help to everyone here, and a great team player. In my past, I have been around many unsavory people and she does not even vaguely resemble them. She loves it here and the guests all love her." As she finished, she teared up.

Gustav and Olive looked at each other in surprise and Gustav said, "We have *no* intention of letting Chef go. We simply need to protect the inn and our guests. Most of all, we wanted to find out if there was anything we could do to help. I agree we have a great team, and see no reason to break it apart."

Now, everyone was crying, and hugging each other. Bambi Lynn finally said, "Well, those rooms won't clean themselves. I better get to it."

Chef Marta agreed, "I still have cleaning to do and then I promised my mother and kids a holiday shopping trip. That is, unless the snow has other plans."

So, everyone went about their day and Gustav and Olive retired to their suite.

Chapter 57:
Jacksonville Jail

Detective Chestnut had been on the phone all morning with other law enforcement agencies. It seemed that Alejandro was wanted by several other counties for a variety of petty crimes, mainly breaking and entering, but still enough to hold him. His court appointed lawyer was meeting with him right then and she awaited the outcome of the interview.

Her assistant, Gary, asked "Do you think there is any way that guy could be involved with the Castleberry disappearance?"

Detective Chestnut answered, "I certainly hope not but I will question him about her. Maybe he stole her car? Or worse?"

They did not have long to wait as his attorney appeared, asking to speak with them. He started, "My client says that nothing happened last night. It was just a disagreement that got out of hand. He is willing to apologize to the maid, and promises not to visit the inn again. When can we expect his release?"

"*Release?*" said Detective Chestnut, incredulously. "He is wanted in several other counties for breaking and entering, petty theft, and a host of others, not to mention he is undocumented. He is here illegally and my guess is that the inn will press charges. He will be here for quite some time in that case as the next court opening is in January."

The attorney seemed somewhat surprised by all of that news, and said he would do some background checking of his own before he would agree to that. He asked for his client to be arraigned on Monday since the judge was not available that day. Detective Chestnut agreed to set it for Monday at 1:00 since that was the first available court time. The attorney then left the station.

Gary said, "I will print out everything I can find on this guy. We can not let him get bail posted because he would flee for certain, and then show up another time, and it would probably be worse. He is quite angry." Detective Chestnut agreed.

Chapter 58:
Sunday evening

Sunday night brought a quiet night by an open fireplace for Gustav and Olive. They discussed the previous few days, and the upcoming community event, caroling and cookies, for which they had many RSVPs. Gustav felt so positive about this event to bring the community together, and have The Mistletoe Inn be the centerpiece. It really was a great idea, and very smart marketing to show the inn with all its holiday décor and welcoming activities. Big snowflakes outside just barely clinging to bare tree branches gave a beautiful winter tableau to anyone who dared a peek from the front door, or an open window.

Back in Dallas, the Castleberry brothers decided they would regroup the following day for lunch and each enjoyed an evening sleeping in their own beds. The snow had blanketed the ground and all the roofs but they hardly noticed as they were both tired, and ready to decompress.

In Oklahoma City, Jeff Willingham had enjoyed some family time that weekend, but now could not think of much else, other than returning to Live Well Pharmaceuticals the following morning to meet with the board, and go over the proposed candidates for the CEO position. Snow coated all the roads, and was still falling, which was winter's reminder that Christmas was near. He also was going to bring up the proposal for first ever Christmas bonuses, and much needed raises, to the board. He felt completely positive about them being the right move to help save the company by dramatically improving morale and loyalty.

Chapter 59:
Scarlett's cell

Scarlett looked out the tiny window to see the beautiful falling snow, and sobbed. She was remembering playing in the snow when she was a young child with her parents, building a snowman, having hot chocolate by the fireplace, and decorating their Christmas Tree. Would she ever be able to make any more Christmas memories? Her attorney felt this was not an impossibility due to the circumstances surrounding the murder, and leading up to the murder. She felt confident he would do his best to get her at least a lighter sentence. Maybe they would even dismiss the charge? No, she musn't get her hopes up on that. It was still murder, not self defense.

After she filled him in on the other guests, he promised to try and speak with each of them on Monday, seeing what they remembered, where they were, if anyone saw anything, etc. He did a good job questioning that lawyer Jeff Willingham. Definitely, he will be called as a witness for her defense. He seemed honest about the other guests, and participating in the ruse to get them together.

Chapter 60: Monday

Monday dawned in Oklahoma City with roads being cleared and traffic moving slowly, but safely. Jeff Willingham made it to Live Well Pharmaceuticals early for his 9:00 board meeting. He wanted to make sure the conference room was ready with agendas for everyone. Then, he went to his office, and awaited their arrival. Everyone made it relatively on time so they did not delay in getting started. Jeff called the meeting to order, and brought up the first item, the replacement of Nigel Fathom.

Each candidate was discussed one at a time and then they held a secret ballot vote for the top three candidates. He counted the ballots and it was almost unanimous. It was going quite well so far. He asked the receptionist to schedule each one for an interview as soon as possible.

Then, for the other items: Christmas bonuses. He brought up this proposal, expecting a push back, but, to his surprise, they unanimously agreed. That would be a much needed morale boost. They suggested a Christmas luncheon, with envelopes being given out on Friday. Agreed. Now, for the last item on his list: much needed raises. He had each department's reviews and the employees' length of service on a spreadsheet. He proposed raises for fifty long time employees who had been overlooked, or just simply ignored. After much discussion on the how and why that happened, the board agreed to the raises. Done! The meeting was adjourned at 12:30, just in time for everyone to go to a quick lunch, and have their afternoon meetings. Jeff closed his door, and breathed a sigh of relief. He had needed that! Now, to make plans for Friday's Christmas luncheon, schedule the raises with human resources, and detail out the Christmas bonuses.

Monday in Jacksonville brought the sun back out but the cold lingering on. It was a typical Texas winter day. With Christmas only a few days away, shoppers rushing around to find yet a few more presents.

At Cyndy's Diner, patrons were buzzing about the missing person's signs everywhere. It seems each person had their own theory about the disappearance. Some wondered if search dogs and psychics could be called in while others just knew she had run away to have some fun, and did not want to be found. Talk quieted down when Detective Chestnut and Gary arrived for an early lunch. They had to be back for the 1:00 arraignment of Alejandro. They were tightlipped about that as they did not want gossip about the case.

At The Mistletoe Inn, RSVPs were flying in for the next evening's carols and cookies. It really was a hit with the townspeople. Gustav was in a great mood as person after person called to say they were coming. Even local favorite Charlotte Champion was coming, and offered to lead the carols! It was going to be the event of the season. With all the town there, what better time to show the inn with its capacity for parties and events? Chef Marta was baking up a storm. She wanted all kinds of treats there to show her expertise, as well as to make the inn a place to book for a shower or party. Bambi Lynn was cleaning every public area to perfection so that it would shine in all its glory.

Across town, Attorney Robert Blake was making call after call to the other guests who were present at The Mistletoe Inn during the murder. He spoke with Dr. Formby first, and found out that he had arrived at the tree trimming event late, with plenty of opportunity to poison Mr. Fathom's coke in the hallway. Of course, Dr. Formby said he never went on the second floor during his stay except when he heard the maid scream. He then ran up the steps to find out what had happened. Dr. Formby said he did not see anyone, or hear anything after the party. He reiterated that he went right to bed, and slept soundly.

Next, he spoke with Lucille Chambers, who claimed she neither saw nor heard anything untoward at the party, nor after the party, but went straight to her room, and fell asleep. He determined she had the least motive of them all. After all, it was her friend who was an employee of Mr. Fathom, not a spouse or child.

When he contacted the famous mystery writer, Raven Du Pree, she was quite forthcoming as she had helped the detective solve the case. They spoke for over an hour, with question after question about motive, opportunity, and the demeanor of each guest. He asked her if she saw or heard anything that night. Yes, she heard sounds but they stopped very quickly so she assumed everything was alright. What did she see? She said she did not tell the detective but she did notice some people seemed to be coming and going during the event. Were they going to the restroom? Were they going to their rooms? She could not be sure, so did not want to share that information. She shared with him all the information she had found about each guest that had pointed to possible motives.

Lastly, he contacted Nancy Ellis. Nancy also had a strong motive since a drug interaction from Live Well Pharmaceuticals had taken the life of her husband. However, she had told everyone her husband was such a kind man that he would not want her to avenge his death. Robert told her he could not imagine her grief over losing him, and to such a preventable cause. He told her he knew that he personally would be so angry that revenge would come very easy. Her room was close to his so she not only had availability, but also the strongest motive, in his mind. He would call her as a witness. Perhaps she would break on the stand.

The other guest was, of course, missing. He found that fact to be quite interesting. By all accounts, she was very angry when all of this was revealed and she tried to deny everything that the detective and Raven du Pree had said. Also, she was overheard threatening the lawyer Jeff Willingham and the inn's owners. Where could she be? Rather convenient. Maybe she was hiding.

Chapter 61:
The Arraignment

Alejandro was arraigned at the Jeffersonville Courthouse at 1:00. His attorney asked for the charges to be dismissed as an unfortunate misunderstanding. But, the prosecutor was ready for that. He had a word with the judge about his being undocumented, and his prior criminal history. The judge agreed, and ordered him remanded to the jail, and to stand trial on January 16th.

Detective Chestnut called The Mistletoe Inn, and let them know the good news. Gustav, Chef Marta, and Bambi Lynn were relieved to hear that news. Hugs were exchanged all around and then they were back to preparing for Tuesday night's event.

Chapter 62:
Monday Evening

Attorney Robert Blake contacted Detective Chestnut, and spoke with her about the disappearance of Renata Castleberry. She assured him their office was doing everything in their power to locate Renata, and had searched repeatedly themselves. They had put out a silver alert, which normally gets attention and tips on the missing, but that was not the result in this case. Nothing. It is like she just disappeared.

He asked her, "Do you think it is possible that she disappeared on purpose?"

Detective Chestnut answered, "Yes, of course, but her sons believe that is impossible."

Hmmmm, he thought. Another road to explore.

In Oklahoma City, Jeff Willingham could not wait to go home, and tell his wife the good news of the board meeting that day, and all the positive things that came out of it. First of all, his time at the company would soon come to a close and he could go back to his normal law practice. Secondly, he felt so good about the positive changes he was able to enact in that short period of time, which should have lasting results. They spent a quiet evening watching a Christmas special.

In Dallas, the brothers came to the conclusion that they would just have to wait and see in the case of their mother's disappearance. It was a somber meeting but they both agreed they had exhausted all the normal means of locating someone. Now, they must wait, and hope for an explanation soon. They discussed every possible scenario, both good and bad, and determined that did them no good. But, at some point, they both agreed that they would have to get a message to their dad in prison. Neither boy had visited him. They simply could not bring themselves to go to the prison. They knew he had kept up with Renata with letters. So, they could get a message to him somehow. But, they would wait a while longer.

Chapter 63:
Tuesday

Tuesday in Dallas was seasonably cold but sunny. The perfect Christmas weather in Texas. Charles awoke with a strange feeling that something was going to happen, a premonition maybe. He rarely had those, but did recognize them. He chose to keep it to himself just in case he was wrong. No reason to alarm anyone else.

It was also beautiful in Jeffersonville as the inn was abuzz with all the preparations for that night's caroling and cookies. Gustav and Olive were thrilled and excited to welcome all their friends and neighbors for this most wonderful time together. The smells from Chef Marta's kitchen were amazing and it was making all of them hungry. She would not let them taste as the food was for the guests. They were to not to arrive until 7:00 but she wanted everything ready!

Oklahoma City weather was much colder, but sunny as well. All the snow melting made driving much easier, and not treacherous. Malls and shops were crowded with last minute shoppers purchasing gifts for family and friends. When Jeff arrived at Live Well Pharmaceuticals, he was greeted warmly. News had traveled fast and, though the holiday plans were all something new to the employees, they were very excited. Just wait until we hand out these bonuses, Jeff thought. Jeff, himself, was personally writing all the checks because he wanted it to be a complete surprise. For the luncheon, he had menus he was contemplating today, would make his final decision, and then let it be known what they could expect as far as food so they could be prepared.

Tuesday afternoon, the tables were being set in the inn to welcome all the guests with a smorgasbord of treats. Every detail was being attended to. Then, they simply had to dress the part, and be ready to show the town The Mistletoe Inn at her finest.

Detective Chestnut and Gary were looking forward to going to this fun event, minus a crime scene. Truth be told, Gary could hardly wait to see Bambi Lynn again. Maybe he could find some mistletoe to steal a kiss under? Without a murder, of course.

Attorney Robert Blake was going over all that he had learned the previous day, and found several areas he wanted discussed in court. He was going to visit Scarlett that day, and would try to keep her as positive as possible since she was spending the Christmas holiday in jail. He still felt unsure about that missing guest, Renata Castleberry. He needed to ask Scarlett about her, what she remembered, what she was like, etc. When he arrived at the jail, Detective Chestnut and Gary were about to take off. He greeted them and they informed him they were going to The Mistletoe Inn for the carols and cookies event. They suggested that he could join them after visiting Scarlett as it did not start until 7:00. He agreed, deciding it might be a great idea to see the full layout of the inn for himself.

Chapter 64:
Sighting

Michelle, a local dog walker, was listening to her playlist as she walked her dog along the shores of Caddo Lake. The weather was great for a walk and there were just a handful of fishermen; no caravans or crowded camp sites. She was glad to be alone on her walk as she could just enjoy the trees and scenery, unlike anywhere else. They had just crossed under the bridge, and were walking along when, out of the corner of her eye, she caught a glimpse of something red in the lake. What was it? She got closer to the water, and still could not really tell what it was, but knew it did not belong here. She decided to call Grady, a local fisherman, to see if he was out that day, and tell him about the strange find.

Michelle began, "Grady? Hey, this is Michelle. Are you out on the lake today?"

Grady replied, "No. Had some things to do in town. Why? Are you?"

Michelle answered, "I'm walking my dog and I am looking at something odd in the lake. Not sure what it is but it is red, and does not belong there. Just was going to see if you could check it out. Probably nothing, but you never know. It could be something important. "

Grady asked, "Where exactly are you?"

Michelle answered, "Close to Hidden Cove."

Grady said, "Okay, I got nothing better to do. I will meet you there in a few minutes."

Michelle replied, "Thanks, Grady. I just know this is something, not just trash."

By that time, t, dusk was settling in. Michelle wrapped up her parka and she and her dog waited for her friend, Grady. Within thirty minutes, he arrived with his bass boat on the trailer.

Michelle pointed the object out to Grady and he agreed it was truly odd. He launched the boat, had her stay on the shore, and motored out to the red object. As he approached, he can see more clearly. It was a submerged car. He could not tell the make or model because only a bit was visible but he did know that he needed to call 911.

It was probably a stolen car or something. Could be a crime…hopefully not. But, either way, he did not want to involve Michelle. So, he went back to shore, and told her it was a car and that he would call the police.

"911. What is your emergency?" asked the operator.

Grady said, "Well, I wouldn't say it is an emergency but there is a red car submerged in Caddo Lake, close to Hidden Cove."

The operator replied, "I have officers on the way. Do not try to enter the car yourself, or pull it up."

Grady said, "No way. I am waiting for help."

Chapter 65:
Carols and Cookies

The Mistletoe Inn was all decked out and the townspeople were all excited. They were arriving all dressed in their holiday attire. Gustav and Olive were greeting them at the door, welcoming them, and Jackson was all set to give tours to anyone who wished to see the different rooms available.

The weather was perfect! Seasonably cold, but no rain or snow. That made for a wonderful evening for a stroll if you were close enoughto walk. Charlottle Champion was all set in the dining room with the piano and selected carols. This was the perfect way to show off the inn during the holidays, and hopefully give the townspeople many ideas for events that could be hosted there.

Chef Marta had outdone herself. There were treats everywhere! There was something for everyone it seemed. She was taking compliments from all who were tasting and Bambi Lynn was cleaning and straightening so there was no mess during this event.

In came Detective Chestnut and Gary, who were welcomed by Gustav and Olive. They went straight to the dining room for the treats. Bambi Lynn was so excited to see Gary not in uniform. He looked even more handsome that night. He flashed her a big smile, and then began to munch on a cookie. Detective Chestnut knew most of the townspeople, and was milling around chatting with everyone.

Attorney Robert Blake came in shortly after and, while Gustav was surprised to see him, he was greeted warmly, and ushered into the dining room as well. He found Detective Chestnut, who was actually glad to see him attend so he could see the layout, and all the atmosphere for himself. She introduced him to Jackson, who had met him briefly before, but was now asked to give Mr. Blake a tour.

Soon, it was time for the carols to begin. Gustav, Olive, and Jackson got the crowd back into the dining room with the piano. Charlotte started them off with a simple one, Jingle Bells, and everyone started singing. That night was one of the Christmas Spirit being celebrated in song and, by joining together, one community. The carols continued with Silent Night, O Little Town of Bethlehem, The First Noel, O Come All Ye Faithful, and they finished off with We Wish You a Merry Christmas. There were so many voices, and such good spirit for all the town to share. Gustav was smiling from ear to ear as this was his dream, sharing his wonderful space with the town of Jeffersonville. He was so happy he and Olive had chosen this place, as they had considered several. This place was so welcoming to newcomers and they quickly felt at home.

Just as people were starting to leave, a deputy came in the door of the inn, looking for Detective Chestnut. He found her and Gary, took them into a quiet nook, and told them about the find in Caddo Lake. They had dispatched a tow truck there to try and raise the red vehicle. Could it be the missing woman's car? It was too early to tell but he knew he needed to inform Detective Chestnut and Gary because of all the searching that had been going on. At that news, she and Gary drove in her car to the lake spot where they were searching. The tow truck was fastening a cable to the car in an attempt to bring it closer to shore.

Once that was done, they began the pull system from the tow truck and, eventually, the red vehicle started moving towards them. It was dark and, until it was very close to shore, you could not begin to see what make/model it was. It was indeed the very same one that Renata had been driving. As the vehicle was hoisted up, a sigh came from both the detective and from Gary. It indeed was Renata's car.

Once the vehicle was at the shore, deputies went, and attempted to see in the windows. Eventually, they were able to get a door open and, when water poured out, there was the missing Renata Castleberry. The next call was to the coroner's office and Detective Chestnut had the deputies place crime scene tape, cordoning off the entire part of the shore where the car was located. What had happened? Was she murdered? It would be a long night, she feared. It was midnight, and the eerie moss-covered cypress trees seemed to fit the investigation quite well.

Then came the task of calling the two sons, and informing them their mother had been located, but was deceased. This was yet another mystery for her and Gary. It was a very good thing that she had not planned to go out of town for the Christmas holiday because it was now looking like she would be tied up in this investigation. Another call would be to Gustav and Olive to inform them of this, once they were certain it was Renata. That could certainly wait until the following as they were all happy tonight because of the great turnout at the carols and cookies event. She wished she had taken some cookies to go. They were so delicious.

Chapter 66:
What was Lost was Now Found

In the early hours of the morning, Detective Chestnut and Gary finally went home to get cleaned up, and meet back at the station. The calls to the two brothers would be next and she certainly was not looking forward to that. It was such a sad part of her job, but entirely necessary. As soon as she arrived back at the station, she immediately went to her desk, and called Charles Castleberry.

She said, "Hello, Mr. Castleberry? This is Detective Chestnut from Jeffersonville calling. Is this a good time to talk?"

Charles agreed and she continued, "We have located your mother and her vehicle, which was in the middle of Caddo Lake. Unfortunately, your mother was deceased and we are awaiting the coroner's report on the exact cause of death at this time. Can we please get you or your brother to come and identify the body? We are also searching the car for any clues and there will be personal effects for you to take as well."

Charles answered, "Yes, of course. Just let me talk to my brother, Michael, and we will be down there as soon as we can. Not sure of his schedule but I am open to leave as soon as possible."

Detective Chestnut answered, "Most certainly. I understand. Would you like me to call Michael?"

Charles answered, "That will not be necessary. I will call him myself, and tell him everything." Charles just hung his head and cried. This was what he had feared most.

They hung up and she knew how awful this scene would be with them coming to identify the body of their mother. No one should have to do that. That was the second worst part of her job; being there during the identification of the body.

Now, to call Gustav at the Inn. He answered. She said, "Gustav, hello. This is Detective Chestnut and I am calling for two reasons. First of all, thank you for a wonderful evening last night. It was just like something out of a Hallmark movie. All the town loved it. Thank you for being such a great community partner. Secondly, I am afraid I have some other news. We have located the missing woman and her car last night, which is why Gary and I left without saying goodbye."

Gustav stammered, "You did?! Where?"

Detective Chestnut replied, "In the middle of Caddo Lake."

Gustav said, "What? Why was she there?"

Detective Chestnut responded, "That is what we will have to find out in the days ahead. She was deceased and I am waiting for the coroner's report to give me a complete cause of death before I speculate. I know the brothers have stayed with you and, since their mother was a guest as well, I thought you would want to know."

Gustav thanked her for the call, and for her kind remarks, and then went to find Olive.

Gustav said, "Olive, they have found Renata Castleberry and her car."

Olive replied, "That is wonderful news! I am certain the boys will be happy to hear that."

Gustav continued, "Olive, her car was in the middle of Caddo Lake and she was dead."

Olive was shocked. "*What*?! Why was she there? What happened? Was she murdered? Oh, no! Another *murder*!" She began to weep. Gustav took her in his arms, and held her. She was so fragile and she needed him to be strong.

Charles Castleberry picked up the phone, and texted Michael to see if they could meet for coffee or lunch. They agreed on their favorite coffee spot at 10:00. When Michael arrived, Charles said, "Michael, Detective Chestnut called this morning and they have found mother and her car."

Michael asked, "How is she. Is she okay? Can we see her?"

Charles put his hand on Michael's arm, and softly said, "No, Michael, she is not okay. They found her in her car in the middle of Caddo Lake. She iss dead. The coroner is working on finding out how she died now. They need us to go to Jeffersonville, identify the body, and get her personal effects as soon as possible."

Michael tried to hold back tears, and finally got up, and went outside the coffee shop. Charles let him have some time, completely understanding, but thinking ahead of everything they would need to do. Since this was the only parent either had ever lost, he did not know exactly what all was involved, but certainly had a good idea.

After a few moments, Michael came back in, and sat down. He said, "Yes, I can take some more time off, and go with you back to Jeffersonville. When did you want to leave?"

Charles answered "This afternoon?" They agreed to drive together, leaving by 2:00 to arrive, and planning to spend one night there to handle everything there, hopefully. Both men went home to pack for an overnight and then Charles picked Michael up and they started on their way.

Chapter 67:
Coroner's Office

The brothers arrived at the coroner's office around 5:00 and Detective Chestnut ushered them in, telling them how sorry she was for their loss. She informed the coroner they were ready to view and their mother's body was wheeled to the window. They uncovered the face and both boys gasped in horror. Her face was distorted, bloated, discolored but it was indeed her.

Detective Chestnut led them out of that area, and proceeded to tell them what she knew so far. The coroner had ruled she died by drowning. There did not seem to be any foul play but her vehicle was still being examined in the event that she may have been forced into the water. The coroner also said she had been in the water for many days, indicating a possible accident the day she left the inn.

The detective hated to ask but, again, it was part of her job. "Do you think there is any possibility that she drove into the lake on purpose?" she asked.

Both brothers together, "*No way!*"

Charles spoke next, "She called us both when she was leaving to say she was looking forward to seeing us, and was planning a possible lawsuit against Live Well Pharmaceuticals for miscarriage of justice against our dad. Why would she say all of that if she was going to commit suicide?"

"Good point," said the detective. "I just had to ask. Now, about your dad... Where is he? He needs to be notified as well."

Michael answered, "In Texarkana in the Federal Correctional Institution. We have not ever been there."

"You have not visited him?" asked the detective.

"No" said both boys emphatically.

Charles added, "He made his choice to steal from the company and he got caught, simple as that. Why should we put ourselves through that nightmare of visiting him in prison?"

"He wrote to us," Michael added.

The detective asked, "Did you mother ever visit him?"

"No, she was too embarrassed," said Charles. "She just would *not* believe that he stole money from the company. She believed him when he told her he was owed that money for bonuses that were never paid."

The detective asked, "Is there any truth to that story?"

Both brothers shook their heads no. Charles continued, "I met with the lawyer, Jeff Willingham, at the Live Well Pharmaceuticals office and he told me the entire story. Dad was caught red handed in the midst of transferring funds from the company into his personal account."

The detective nodded, "Okay, then, we will find a way to have him notified that will not involve you. Next question, do you know your mother's wishes? Did she wish to be buried? Where? Cremated? I know this is hard but you two are now in charge of her body."

The two brothers looked like deer in the headlights at the mention of all of that so she added, "Look, why don't you talk it over amongst yourselves, and let me know?" She shook their hands and off they went.

In the car, the silence was deep. Michael turned on the radio to break it up as they drove to the inn. When they entered the familiar doorway, they were greeted by Gustav. They shook hands, and asked they asked Gustav if he had any rooms available for them.

He said, "Of course. Would you like the same rooms you had before?"

"Yes, please," they both said.

He checked them in, and gave them their keys, taking time to tell them that Detective Chestnut had informed him that morning of the sad discovery and that the staff all were very sorry for the loss of their mother. "Is there anything else we can do for you?" he asked.

The two brothers just hung their heads, and said, "No, thank you," as they headed to their rooms.

Chapter 68:
The Prisoner

The next day, Detective Chestnut asked the chief of police how to go about notifying someone in prison of the death of their spouse. He told her it was a simple phone call to the warden of the prison. So, she took it upon herself to call the warden of the unit in Texarkana where Mr. Castleberry was incarcerated. She informed him of the finding of the body and that drowning was the cause of death. At that time, it appeared to be accidental. She then asked if he would relay that information to Mr. Castleberry. She added that that the sons, Charles and Michael, had identified the body, and were now in charge of planning the disposition of her remains. The warden promised to carry that message directly to the prisoner as soon as possible.

When they hung up, Warden Bill Morris called in his assistant to locate Mr. Castleberry, and bring him into a conference room where he could give him the news. It took quite a while, but, finally, it was accomplished. Mr. Castleberry was informed, and immediately broke down crying.

He kept saying, "This is all my fault…all my fault I just know it." They let him compose himself and then he was taken back to his cell.

The warden thought to himself…*better watch this one. He might take matters into his own hands.*

Chapter 69:
Thursday

The brothers met for breakfast and the staff was very kind and gracious to them. They almost felt like family. Speaking of family, they had much to do. First things first, what to do with her body? Did she have a will? If so, where was it? Who would know that? Only one person, their dad. They could not remember either parent ever mentioning this so how could they know? But, for now, they had to make a quick decision. The easiest thing to do was to have her cremated there, and just bring the ashes back to Oklahoma City for a memorial service. They would check for a will later but, faced with this decision right now, cremation would be their choice.

They called the detective, and let her know of their decision. She then directed them to Peters Funeral Home for that service. They would simply need to pay for the cremation service, and the receptacle for the ashes. They got directions from Gustav and away they went. They had no trouble finding the funeral home, and went inside to make those decisions. There were many choices, even with the choice made for cremation, so that took longer than expected. Eventually, they paid, and went on their way to the police station to find out where they stood with releasing the personal effects.

Detective Chestnut was there, and did have some things for them to see. She took them in a conference room for privacy. She had Renata's purse, luggage, some Christmas presents, still wrapped, her cell phone, and a surprise. It was the envelope like the one Jeff Willingham had given to the other guests as well. The amount was more than enough to cover the cremation and all other expenses for a memorial service in Oklahoma City. Wet, but drying out, it was all there. She was not robbed. It was looking to have been just a terrible accident unless, no, the boys just could not comprehend that. Renata was not totally stable, but suicidal? No way. They would need to let Jeff Willingham know that they did, indeed, find her, and the check, which was now going to pay for her services.

Jeff was getting all the details ready for the Christmas luncheon the following day, as well as signing check after check of Christmas bonuses to be handed out at the luncheon. That's when he received the call from Charles Castleberry. "Hello, how may I help you?" he asked.

Charles answered, "Mr. Willingham, I just called to let you know that we did locate my mother, Renata. It seems there was a terrible accident and her car wound up in Caddo Lake where she drowned. They found the car and her body on Tuesday night and we identified her yesterday. The reason for my call is that the envelope you had given her at The Mistletoe Inn was still with her. The check is certainly wet but the police are trying to save it. We are hoping it would be okay to use the money to pay for her cremation, a receptacle for her ashes, and to set up a memorial service in Oklahoma City in January."

Jeff answered, "Oh, I am so very sorry to hear all of this! Of course, it would be okay. Do you need me to contact the funeral home, and take care of this for you?"

Charles said, "No, thank you. We already gave them a credit card to cover this part in Jeffersonville. But, it would certainly be nice to get reimbursed for this as we have no idea if she had a will, or where it would be. We will look for it when we get to Oklahoma City, which will not be until we have her ashes with us. Also, we need to take care of disposing of the car, call the car insurance company, etc."

Attorney Jeff Willingham felt so sorry for those two brothers shouldering all of this at Christmas time. He made a note to keep up with them for the next few days, and see what he could do to help. After all, now they had a probate issue as well with the house since their dad was not in the picture. He had never encountered anything like this in his career.

After the brothers had a late lunch at the local brewery, they discussed their next move. Michael agreed to call the car insurance company, and give them the news. Detective Chestnut had said her deputy would be happy to speak with them and they would work all of this out. No worries there. That just left their dad. What to do about him? Neither one wanted to see him but they did need to know about a possible will, life insurance, the house. How could they handle all of this on their own? They needed help and he was the only one who could answer all of those questions. They agreed to sleep on it, and decide the next morning what to do.

It was dark when they arrived back at The Mistletoe Inn. They were tired and they just went to their rooms.

Chapter 70:
Friday

Morning arrived, dark and dreary. Winter was indeed in full swing. The boys thought this fitting for the decision they had made, with much consternation, to visit their dad in prison. Charles called Detective Chestnut to see how to arrange this. She promised to set up a visit as soon as possible.

Detective Chestnut called Warden Morris again, and asked if it would be possible for the two sons to visit their dad, in view of the circumstances. They needed to ask him all sorts of questions that only he would know. Warden Morris felt this was indeed a special circumstance, and told her it would be okay but, obviously, supervised. They would be thoroughly searched and they must agree to the rules of the prison. No touching; only talking. No gifts and nothing on their persons allowed. She agreed to go over that with them. Warden Morris agreed for a time on Saturday during visiting hours.

Detective Chestnut went to the inn to visit with the boys, and told them all the details involved in visiting a prisoner. They were immediately nervous, but did agree there did not seem to be any other way. So, they had to prepare for the following day's visit. They agreed to develop an agenda for the visit, covering all the questions they needed answered. Detective Chestnut thought this a very good plan. Then, she said goodbye, and went back to the station.

Friday in Oklahoma City was also dreary but Jeff Willingham was all smiles as he arrived at the office. He knew that his surprise with the Christmas bonuses would be a much-needed holiday treat for all of the employees, and would be a positive way to head into Christmas week. He checked with human resources, and the admins. Everything for the luncheon was in place. The caterer would be there by 11:00 to set up the food table and they had agreed on a strategy to have a serving line and multiple tables where employees could sit and eat. Then, Jeff would make the announcement of the Christmas bonuses while he was thanking the employees for a great year, and telling them that they would soon have a new CEO. The interviews would be conducted starting the following week.

The luncheon was a huge success and the announcement of the bonus was a hit! Applause filled the air, just as Jeff had figured.

As each employee left, the bonuses were handed to each one personally. Each employee shook his hand, and thanked him for the wonderful surprise. When everyone had left, Jeff checked with human resources to see about the upcoming interviews, and then went home to his family. They were going to have a wonderful, much-needed family weekend of holiday activities.

Attorney Robert Blake was hard at his defense strategy. After taking a tour of the inn on Tuesday, he then spent Wednesday and Thursday going over the interviews of each of the other four guests, including Raven Du Pree. Unfortunately, yesterday, he'd found out that the fifth guest, Renata Castleberry, had been found deceased. Could she have been a suspect? *Yes* and she certainly had a great motive. He would have to explore all of those motives and characters, and come up with the best plan possible to convince a jury that Scarlett Johnson was not guilty of murder.

Detective Chestnut was called to forensics to check out Renata's vehicle herself. They had found something that may indicate her death was more than an accidental slide off the road. When she arrived, the techs showed her some damage on the left rear of the car, seeming to show it received quite the hit at some point.

When she spoke with the insurance adjustor, he was as surprised as she was about the damage. It had not ever been reported and there was not another scratch or dent on the entire car. They were hard at work trying to figure out how the damage could have happened. It appeared that someone hit Renata's vehicle quite hard on the left rear. If, indeed, she was just at the edge of the bridge, that force could have knocked her car down the embankment, and into the water below, water that was swift-moving, and quite deep at that point.

The accident team was going to visit the bridge on both ends, and see if they could find *any* evidence of that happening. Detective Chestnut was very interested in that finding as it could give the boys some closure. It would take quite a while to determine, so, for now, she decided not to say anything to the boys.

Back at the station, the court appointed lawyer for Alejandro was visiting his client, but wished to have a word with the detective afterwards. He had found out the petty crimes that his client had committed, and was hoping for a plea deal. Detective Chestnut asked the prosecutor to join them, and was enlightened to find out that Alejandro stole a car, which was later abandoned, with his fingerprints all over it. The car had sustained quite a bit of damage as he apparently had hit someone from behind quite hard, like he was trying to pass them on the left. The damage was to the front center and right of the car. Hmmm… Could it be?

Detective Chestnut asked the prosecutor to step out into the hallway, and told him what she was thinking. Could Alejandro have tried to pass Renata on that bridge, hit her quite hard, and forced her car down an embankment into the water below? She told him to stall any talk of a plea deal until the accident team came back with their report. Also, she asked him to check the dates and time of the reported theft, and the abandonment of the car. Where was it found? How was it found?

Back at The Mistletoe Inn, the brothers were planning on a quiet evening, maybe a pizza and a couple of beers, when Cyndy of Cyndy's Diner stopped by with dinner for them, with her sincere condolences. She was accompanied by several other townspeople who had brought desserts, appetizers, and drinks. They all expressed their sorrow at the news of Renata's passing, and wanted to show them that they felt they were family there. There was so much food that Gustav invited them all to stay, and eat, together in the dining room to help cheer them up..

This was exactly what the two brothers needed and Gustav and Olive were so proud of their community for stepping up to help them with their grief. Stories were shared and, by the time everyone left, they indeed felt better, and like family. When they went to their rooms, they were so thankful that they had come to know those people, and saw what Gustav and Olive had found there, a wonderful, caring community that took care of each other.

Chapter 71:
The Visit

Saturday dawned cold and cloudy, but not dreary like the previous day. It was perfect for what lay ahead for Charles and Michael. They met in the dining room, ate a quick breakfast, and got on the road to Texarkana for the task of visiting their dad in prison. It was a three-hour drive so they had plenty of time to talk about what they were going to say, what questions they had, and about their feelings of anxiety towards seeing him again.

They were going to ask about the existence of a will, a funeral plot, and the house situation, as well as talking about Renata, and how she was feeling the day the accident happened. Their dad needed to know that. Both of them were adamant that they wanted him to suffer in this case. In their mind, all of this was because of him. If he had not done what he did, Renata would not have been invited to that weekend, would not have met those other people, would not have been so upset, and would not have died.

They drove up to the facility and a guard house was where they were instructed to stop. They were told where to park, and how to proceed with the other families who were gathering to visit their incarcerated loved ones. The process was so severe, with so many searches, and physical check points, that anyone would be nervous by the time they were allowed in. The boys were taken to a locked room with a guard while another guard went to get their dad.

When he was led into the room, they hardly recognized him. He had aged so much, and looked so severe, that they almost felt sorry for him. Almost, but not, as they were resolute in their emotions towards him, and what his crime had done to their family. He immediately teared up seeing them, and asked them how they were doing. He then kept crying as he said how sorry he was about Renata and that he knew it was all his fault. He asked them if they knew any more about what had happened. All of that happened before theys could ask about everything they needed to know.

Charles took charge, and started, asking their dad, "Did she have a will?"

Their dad shook his head, no.

Charles continued, "What should we do with the house? Is it paid for?"

Their dad answered, "Yes, son. The house is all paid for. What do you want to do with it?"

Charles answered, "We need to sell it because it is just sitting there vacant. But, now, without a will, we will have to go through the legal process and a judge will determine what happens."

Their dad answered, "Yes, I guess that is what has to happen. I should have managed our situation, and protected us, but…"

Michael interrupted him, "But, you *didn't*! Instead, you put us all in this terrible situation and now *we* have to deal with all of it."

Charles tried one more question as their dad was now sobbing. "Did she have any life insurance?"

Again, their dad shook his head. "Not that I know of. I am so, so sorry. I hope that one day you can forgive me for all of this."

At that point, they were done, and motioned for the guard that they were ready to go.

After they got back to their car, after retrieving their personal effects from the guards, they started back to Jeffersonville, very somber indeed. The visit had only confirmed what they were afraid of. Their dad had not managed anything for them. They were now in charge of handling it all.

They stopped for lunch on the road, neither of them very hungry, but dreading the long trip back. Now what? They really needed advice. It seemed they needed to talk with Detective Chestnut again. They trusted her and she would know what they needed to do.

After they got back in the car, they drove straight back to Jeffersonville, and to the police station, hoping to find her. Unfortunately, she had gone for the weekend but they left a message for her to contact them on Monday morning.

They then visited the funeral home to see when they could pick up Renata's ashes. They were promised everything would be ready on Monday. So, it seemed they will be in Jeffersonville that night, and the following day as well. Well, at least they were not alone. They felt they had family there.

Chapter 72:
Sunday

On Sunday, the accident team and the insurance adjustor were convening to try to recreate the accident, and determine exactly what had happened. Detective Chestnut had alerted them to the stolen car incident that had a possible link to Renata's death. They had located the car, checked the damage, and were using computer models to see exactly how it could have happened. A team on the bridge had seen some swerve marks on one end. They were trying to get the pieces to fit. Even though she was with family for the weekend, the detective asked to be kept in the loop because this case was now very much at the top of her agenda.

On Sunday, in Oklahoma City, Jeff Willingham could not help but think about those two young men and what they would be facing legally and emotionally while dealing with the court process of probate. As he sat in church, he said a prayer for them, and wished there was something he could do to help.

Sunday at the inn was quiet. It was Christmas week and they had guests coming in on Christmas Eve, and staying through New Years Day. Gustav and Olive were planning everything for those four guests, and wondering about the brothers. They hated for them to return to Dallas alone if they had no family to spend Christmas with. Olive suggested they ask them who they were going to spend Christmas with, and offer (for free) for them to spend Christmas week at the inn. Financially, they could afford it and they felt it a very positive thing to do. They agreed that, on Monday morning, they would mention it to them, and then, if they said yes, they would tell Cyndy, Detective Chestnut, and others close to them. All in all, it was a cold, blustery, quiet day, best kept indoors, close to the fireplace. They enjoyed hot chocolate, cookies, and popcorn.

The brothers had not slept well as the visit upset them. It brought back all the bad memories of before, when the crime was exposed and their dad was arrested, the trial, and his being sentenced to federal prison for embezzlement. Renata refused to believe it, and became a recluse after federal agents raided their home, and took many things away that had been bought with stolen money from Live Well Pharmaceuticals. Try as they might, they could not get her to face reality; that her husband was a criminal behind bars and that she was not going to get her old life back.

When they finally met in the dining room around 1:00, they decided to go out to the brewery, have a couple of beers and a sandwich, and write down all the questions for Detective Chestnut about their situation. What would they do first? What did the probate process entail? What information did they need? Also, they realized that the process would require an attorney. They discussed who to hire. Obviously, the only attorney in Oklahoma City they knew at all was Jeff Willingham. He did say he would be glad to help but they were not sure if he meant legally.

Neither of them was in any hurry to go back to the inn. So, they decided to look around at the shops, and see if they found anything interesting. They found some interesting facts in the court house. There even was an old prison, which had housed many infamous characters at one time. They toured the museum, and found a pie place that served the biggest slices of pie they had ever seen. Christmas music was playing everywhere and their moods were lightening as they were exploring. It was dark by the time they returned to the inn. The family had retired to their suite so they both went to their rooms, and called it a night.

Chapter 73:
Monday of Christmas Week

Monday morning, the two brothers felt rested, and ready for the answers they needed. When they met for breakfast, Gustav and Olive asked them about their Christmas week plans. When they answered that they had none, the Boudreaux's asked them to stay for free until the day after Christmas, and enjoy the holiday week with them. It would just be a few more days and maybe it would make them feel better.

Charles and Michael were shocked and, after looking at one another, heartily accepted. They would stay there until Thursday. After all, it did feel like home.

After breakfast, they headed to the police station to meet with Detective Chestnut. They had all their questions ready, and, hopefully, would walk away with some answers. As they entered the station, they saw Gary, who greeted them, and led them to a conference room to wait for the detective. When she came in the door, she had a smile on her face as she had some very important news for them.

"Hello there, you two. I have some important news for you that may help give you some closure" she began. "The accident investigation team determined your mother's car had sustained some damage on the rear and the insurance adjustor was quite surprised. It seems the car was immaculate in every other way, making that an anomaly. Around that time, there came to my attention the report of a stolen car that was found abandoned on that same day. It, too, sustained damage, but on the front. The paint seems to match and we feel now that the person in the stolen car was trying to pass her on the bridge over Caddo Lake when he hit her for whatever reason. The hit must have caused her to veer off the road as there are some swerve marks there. It would have been slick due to the rain that day. Her car simply slid down the embankment, under the bridge, and into the deepest water of the lake which is also swift-moving and dangerous," she finished.

Charles answered, "*Wow*! So, she did not do anything intentional or crazy, but was forced off the road by someone in a stolen car? Did he not stop? No, I guess that, if he had stolen a car, the last thing he would do is stop, especially if he thought he'd committed another crime."

"Exactly," said Detective Chestnut.

"How did you find all of this?" Charles asked.

"We have him in custody for another case, were checking into any other possible charges, and it just fell into the timeframe. His fingerprints are all over the stolen car and the rest was due to the accident team's thorough investigation," Detective Chestnut answered.

Michael said, "Now what? Will he be charged for her death?"

"Yes, manslaughter will be added to his charges today," Detective Chestnut answered. She continued, "He will go away for quite a while now, and will not be able to hurt anyone else. You see, we arrested him at the inn when he had come to extort money from Chef Marta. He knows her cousin and she had helped him before. It is a long, detailed story but we've got him now."

Charles asked, "The Mistletoe Inn?"

"Yes," answered the detective.

Charles continued, "That is incredible! What a crime spree that person caused!"

"Yes," agreed the detective. "Now, what can I do to help you two? You must have come to see me for a reason. How did the visit go with your dad?" she asked.

The two brothers went over the visit with her, and told her they were done with him, and did not ever wish to go there again. He was of no help to them at all and they were starting to believe that he never was. She was so sad for them at hearing this, although not totally surprised.

"We need to know about what we need to do next. Apparently, we have to go through the probate process to deal with the house. Do you know anything about that?" asked Charles.

"Yes. Unfortunately, I had to go through that with the death of my grandmother because I lived with her during college, and afterward during my police academy days," she confided. "You will need to find an attorney to help you with this. Do you know of anyone there?"

Charles answered, "Only that Jeff Willingham. Do you think that it would be okay to ask him since he was the lawyer who helped put our dad in prison?"

She thought for a minute, and said, "That would be an interesting thought. Not sure if that might be a conflict of interest, though. No harm in asking him."

They knew she had many other things to do so they said goodbye, except to tell her they had decided to stay through Christmas.

She was happy to hear that as she had grown quite fond of them, and did not want them to be alone for the holiday. She decided to tell a few people so that, maybe, they could include them with any holiday celebrations.

Next, they headed to the funeral home. They arrived and, as promised, they were handed, after signing a few documents, Renata's ashes in an urn to take home. The boys thanked them for taking care of her, and left. It was then past time for lunch so they headed downtown. They wanted to try somewhere quiet so they found a little Mexican restaurant where they could talk over all that had happened that morning. It was all quite a revelation. In a way, it made both of them feel better. In another way, it made them angry that a criminal had done that to Renata. But, they were assured the detective was going to make certain that he spent time behind bars, rather than get a chance to hurt someone else.

Chapter 74: Alejandro

Alejandro had been in jail for five, almost six days. He did not understand what was taking so long. His lawyer should have gotten the charges dropped by now. That detective has it in for him but she did not know that he had very powerful friends in Mexico that would not let the situation proceed, surely, after all he had done for them. He almost laughed at that thought.

His lawyer was scheduled to visit him again that day and he was going to demand he be released, or else. It probably would not be too hard to bribe a guard to let him make one phone call to Mexico. Then, they would see! He would wreak havoc on them like never before for this mistreatment and he would start with that uppity Marta. She would pay for sure!

Just after lunch, his lawyer appeared, and asked for a meeting. He told Alejandro that, not only was he not being released, but that the charges were heaping up on him and his only hope was a plea bargain. As he explained, in Spanish, what that would mean, Alejandro got furious, and started yelling and cursing at him. The lawyer told him that he did not have to take that treatment, and left.

Alejandro just could not believe it! That clown just told him he was going to prison. The only thing he could do is negotiate a deal for a lesser sentence. That couldn't be right. He just needed to think, and devise a plan. What information could he use to help himself? How about telling them of Marta's husband's whereabouts in Mexico? Maybe that would help. He asked the guard if he could get some time with the detective's assistant, Gary. Maybe he would listen.

Later that day, Gary came to the cell, and brought an interpreter with him. Alejandro played nice, and said he had information that they probably would want, but would only give it if it helped him. He wanted to be released. When Gary heard this, he just laughed, and said that would not be happening. Alejandro got angry, and verbally abusive again. Gary and the interpreter left.

Alejandro's lawyer was in with the prosecutor when he was informed of the new charge leveled against his client, manslaughter. He was shocked, and did not know what to say as the prosecutor detailed out the evidence, adding that there would be *no* plea deal offer. Alejandro would stand trial for all of the charges, and would be going to prison. The attorney was to inform Alejandro that he would be arraigned on the new charges later that day; the car theft, and manslaughter for running Renata off the road, causing her death.

So, he went back to the cell to inform Alejandro of the developments. As expected, that certainly does not go well. He turned to leave, and said, "I will see you in court."

Alejandro did not know what to say. How could this be? What were they talking about? He remembered bumping a car in the rain when he was passing some lady driving all over the road, but…causing her death? He'd never killed anyone, at least none that he knew about.

Chapter 75:
Chef Marta

Shortly after the brothers left the police station, Detective Chestnut went to see Chef Marta at The Mistletoe Inn. She had finished cleaning up, and was working on her plan for the week as the detective came in. Marta was surprised to see her, and asked her to sit down.

Marta was nervous. What had happened? Detective Chestnut informed her of the new charges against Alejandro and that he would definitely be going to prison. The only question was for how long?

Chef Marta started to cry and Detective Chestnut got her some tissues. She actually thought the Chef would be relieved. When she could talk, Marta said how sorry she was about him since he was technically family. She told the detective that he worked for very bad people, crime bosses in Mexico, who had used him for many things over the years, none of them good. But, still, to cause the death of that lady? That was horrible, even for him. She said she felt so bad about that and about those two young men losing their mother.

Detective Chestnut then told her that they did know that as they had come to see her about what to do that morning and she told them. She said they certainly would not blame her in any way. She then told Chef Marta she needed to get back to the police station as there were many details about this case that needed to be wrapped up. Chef Marta thanked her for coming to see her, and for her understanding.

When Detective Chestnut left, Chef Marta knew she needed to get word to her husband about this as she certainly did not want those bosses going to him about Alejandro. As soon as she could go, she left to go and place a call to Mexico, to her husband.

Chapter 76:
Alejandro's Arraignment

Later that afternoon, Alejandro was brought before the judge again. He was facing additional charges for vehicular manslaughter, theft of a vehicle, failure to stop and render aid, and more. His lawyer really could not say much, except that, with the weather conditions that day, his client may not have realized how serious the bump to the car in front of him was. The judge claimed that was of no interest to him, and remanded Alejandro to await trial in the Jeffersonville Jail as he was a flight risk, and an organized crime risk as well.

When all of that was translated to Alejandro, he knew he needed help from his bosses in Mexico. How could he get a message to them? His appointed lawyer was a joke and he needed real help from someone who knew their business. As he sat, and thought, he wondered if he could get a message to Marta for her husband to get help. He needed a plan…

Chapter 77: Jeff Willingham

Later that afternoon, the brothers placed a call to Jeff Willingham. They wanted to let him know about the cause of their mother's death, the visit with their dad, and about how they could proceed in dealing with the house.

Jeff answered, "Hello, how may I help you?"

Charles responded, "Mr. Willingham, it is Charles and Michael Castleberry with news and questions. Is this a good time to talk?"

Jeff answered, "Yes, it is. What has happened?"

The two brothers,, on speaker phone, proceeded to tell him all that had happened from that day's news, the prison visit, and finding out they are at square one, with no will and no plan.

Charles asked, "Can you help us? We know we need an attorney and you are familiar with all of this."

Jeff answered, "Yes, I will try my best but you need to understand this is not a quick-fix situation. We will need to have papers signed by your dad, and filed with the court here and then we can start the probate process. That could take weeks or months, depending on the court docket, and how fast we can get the documents signed and witnessed."

They sighed and Charles said, "Okay. Just tell us what we need to do to facilitate this situation. Does it make any difference since her death is now tied to a court case?"

Jeff answered, "It shouldn't but let me talk to the detective on the case, and find out. Also, since this is a holiday week, I'm not sure how much I can do this week or next, really. Probably not much can be done until January, realistically."

They reluctantly agreed to just wait until Jeff got back to them with a plan after he spoke with Detective Chestnut. Jeff wanted to help them. He felt so bad about the situation even though, as he kept reminding himself, their dad was the one who put his family in the situation.

Chapter 78:
Monday Night

As the two brothers made their way back to the inn, the news had already reached Gustav and Olive. Now, on top of planning a memorial, and everything else that goes with the closing of an estate, they found out that their mother was run off the road by a criminal in a stolen car. Gustav and Olive could not help but feel such sympathy for the two. Since they did not have any other guests that evening, they decided to have a nice night in front of the fireplace with pizzas and Christmas movies, in the hopes that would help them temporarily forget their situation. Jackson joined them as well and they agreed, grateful for the distraction.

The next day would be Christmas Eve. They would have four new guests arriving and there would be a traditional Christmas Eve candlelight service at the Methodist Church nearby, with carols, and a nativity scene. Hopefully, it would bring some peace and hope to the young men for a resolved situation, sooner rather than later, and a much better new year.

Chapter 79:
The Dad

When Jeff Willingham called the federal prison in Texarkana late Monday afternoon, and spoke with Warden Morris, he told him that the brothers had contacted him to help them close out the estate of their mother. told him the new information about the cause of her death, and asked what forms he would need signed for them to be able to conduct a probate, and release the house to the boys for their managing.

Warden Morris thought about that, and sent for their dad to tell him the news personally. He seemed to take it in stride, offering to sign anything that would help them since all of it was his fault. He was emotional after finding out the cause of Renata's death, especially that the criminal did not try to help her as her car went into the lake. But, seemed resigned to his fate, being estranged totally from his sons, as they wished.

Later, after he was returned to his cell, he sobbed, and decided what to do to make this easier for all concerned. Now, to carry out his plan. First, he needed to write a note.

Chapter 80:
Christmas Eve

Christmas Eve was a beautiful, seasonably cold day that was as perfect as it could be. Chef Marta had made some wonderful treats and the two young men, as well as Gustav, Olive, and Jackson, all enjoyed them.

Olive discussed the candlelight service scheduled for that night and the brothers agreed to accompany them. They excused themselves after breakfast, and decided to shop for Gustav, Olive, Jackson, Chef Marta, and Bambi Lynn, as well as Detective Chestnut and Gary for showing them such kindness during the past month. The shops downtown were busy with the very last-minute shoppers who were all trying to find that perfect gift. Shopping was a distraction and, soon, they found themselves hungry, and stopped at Cyndy's for a bite. There, they found many friendly townspeople who wished them well, treated them for lunch, and promised to see them at the candlelight service that night.

Michael and Charles had never experienced anything like that before where the entire community comes together to help someone, even strangers. It was truly inspiring and they would not soon forget it. It truly made their situation a little more bearable.

When they finished their shopping, it was late afternoon. They got back to the inn, kept the gifts in their rooms as surprises, changed clothes, and prepared to join the others for the candlelight service, not knowing what to expect.

When they arrived at the church, everyone was there, waving and offering Merry Christmas greetings, and even hugging them, which felt amazing to them. The service itself was beautiful, and very moving, and ended in candlelight with the singing of Silent Night. It was truly a beautiful way to end the evening but, as they found their way back to the inn, a crowd awaited them and, again, there were townspeople coming to wish them well, hug them, and share Christmas treats with them. It was a magical evening; one right out of a Hallmark movie.

The brothers went to their rooms feeling loved, and cared for, like they had not felt in a very long time.

Chapter 81:
Christmas Eve at the Prison

Christmas Eve brought some better food. Some group usually came to entertain for a few moments but, otherwise, in prison, it is just another day. Harold Castleberry had made his decision the previous day, after contemplating it since Renata's death. He was writing his note, and devising his plan of action to make life easier for his sons. When it came time for sleeping, he executed his plan, leaving his note on his bed.

When the guard came by later that night to check on the prisoners, everything looked normal. The plan worked.

Chapter 82:
Christmas Day

Christmas morning dawned beautifully with not a cloud in the sky. It truly was wonderful. As the brothers made their way into the dining room, they put their gifts under the big Christmas tree so that they would be found later. The new guests were having breakfast and Chef Marta had outdone herself. The spread was truly amazing! Mimosas were served, as well as coffee and tea, and the guests were thrilled at all the holiday treats.

Gustav and Olive addressed the dining room, along with Jackson, Chef Marta, and Bambi Lynn, making a Christmas toast, and wishing everyone a merry Christmas from The Mistletoe Inn. They all sang a couple of carols, and then finished their feasts. The four new guests all had places to be so they left first, leaving the Charles and Michael with the staff. Now was the time. The two brothers went, and got their presents, presenting them one at time to each of the staff, thanking them for all of their kindnesses, and for making them truly feel like family!

There were tears and laughter as all the gifts were opened, and hugs for both of the boys. It actually felt like Christmas should feel. Chef Marta hugged them both, thanking them for their kindness towards her. There was a knock at the door and Cyndy of Cyndy's Diner came in with several of the townspeople, bringing treats to share. They had all wanted to see them on Christmas. They brought Christmas crackers, played games, ate more treats, shared stories, and, in general, had a wonderful Christmas day. They stayed until everyone was full of treats and joy. Then, they filtered out.

Gary came with a special present for Bambi Lynn. She was so surprised and thrilled! She thanked him with a kiss under the mistletoe. The young men gave Gary their gift, after taking a photo of the two lovebirds.

After everyone had left, Detective Chestnut appeared. She asked to speak with the brothers privately so they went to the front parlor. She informed them of a phone call she received from Warden Morris at the federal prison that afternoon. When the cell block lined up for breakfast that morning, their dad did not get up from his bed. Upon checking in his cell, he was found unresponsive, and later declared dead.

There was a note on his body, addressed to Charles and Michael. It simply said, "I am sorry for everything. This should make your lives easier. Check in the bureau at home for my life insurance policy, which is paid up. Love, Dad."

The two did not know what to say. Waves of emotion came and went. Detective Chestnut apologized for the timing of the news, but did not know when they planned on leaving. They hugged her, and gave her their present.

They were stunned, to say the least, but did agree on one thing. It avoided one problem. But, did it create others? Only a lawyer would know. The following day, they would need to head to Oklahoma City for two reasons. They found Gustav, and informed him they would be leaving the next morning after breakfast. Sleep would not come easily for either of them but they both retreated to their rooms to pack.

Chapter 83:
Chef Marta

When Chef Marta got home to celebrate Christmas with her family, she got the surprise of her life. Her husband was there! They hugged, and cried and she kept asking, "How are you here? What if they find you?" She then kept on hugging him tightly.

He said he had come with someone in the dark of night who had business there.

"Who?" she asked.

He replied that it would be better if she did not ask too many questions. He could only stay one day, and wanted to make the most of it. They spent the day loving on each other and the kids. It truly was a magical Christmas.

Then, as Marta slept, her husband crept out the door to meet his transport. He left her a present on his pillow, and promised that he would return when he could clear his name.

Chapter 84:
Christmas in the Jeffersonville Jail

The prisoners were treated to a Christmas dinner from Cyndy's Diner, courtesy of Cyndy herself. That was highly unusual, but very welcome.

During the day, as expected, family came to visit their loved ones. Even Alejandro had a visitor; a family member. He did not stay long, and was watched by a guard who only allowed it because it was Christmas Day. The guard did not notice the look on Alejandro's face when his visitor got up to leave. Later that evening, as the shifts were changing, a new face came on duty but no one seemed to notice. He went to see Alejandro during the night, and acted quickly, and quietly. He then left during his break time, not seen by anyone. His mission was complete.

Chapter 85:
December 26

Breakfast came early in the jail so, when Alejandro did not move when he was told to do so, the guard went in to check on him. Alejandro had been stabbed in the heart, and had died instantly, according to the doctor who was called immediately.

When Detective Chestnut arrived at the police station, she was immediately informed of Alejandro's death. She knew she needed to talk to Chef Marta so she went straight to The Mistletoe Inn.

Chef Marta was busy with breakfast but Bambi Lynn took over for her so she could talk with the detective. When she was informed of the death, she immediately started sobbing. "Too much death!" she kept repeating. She finally composed herself, and went back into the kitchen to finish serving the guests.

Detective Chestnut found that odd but, under the circumstances, all of it was.

Back at the police station, a locked supply closet was opened, only to find another body. It was a guard who had been knocked unconscious, undressed, bound, and gagged. Unfortunately, he was dead by the time he was located. That could possibly explain the death of Alejandro, but who did this? Why was he killed? It was even worse to find out that it was Joe, who had agreed to fill in on Christmas Day, and was set to retire in January. Joe was 67, much loved by everyone in the department, and had just lost his wife the previous year.

Charles and Michael were packed, and ready to leave as soon as they had finished breakfast. They noticed Detective Chestnut leaving the inn, and wanted to say goodbye. She pulled them aside, and gave them the news about Alejandro.

Wow! No one saw that coming. She hugged them both, and wished them all the best in straightening out the estates of both parents, and the upcoming probate process.

As she was leaving, she was thinking this truly was the most twisted case ever. Starting with a murder at this charming bed and breakfast, and ending with all those deaths. Now, it seemed the trail was cold, unless something or someone came forward. It looked like a professional hit. Hmmm… Maybe his crimes were not so petty after all. Maybe he knew too much, and was a loose end to the crime bosses he worked for. The *only* person who could possibly shed some light on the situation was in Mexico, Chef Marta's husband. Maybe that was why she was so upset at the news that morning.

When the detective arrived back at the police station, she was informed of the guard's death. Then, she was convinced that this was a professional and it probably came from the Mexican crime boss. She needed to speak to her chief, and ask his opinion on how to proceed with the situation.

Chapter 86:
Oklahoma, Here We Come

Charles and Michael said their goodbyes to the staff of The Mistletoe Inn, and headed on the road to Oklahoma City. It was a six-hour drive they were not looking forward to but it was certainly necessary. There was so much to do. First, to visit the house, and check the bureau for the life insurance their dad had mentioned in his last words. Second, to call attorney Jeff Willingham, inform him of all the news, and see when they could get an appointment with him to get the paperwork started for the probate process. Also, what to do with their dad's body? They certainly wanted him cremated, but were not sure how to arrange that since he died in prison. Surely, Jeff would know what to do.

Then, they would need to get the house ready to sell. Neither of them wanted to move to Oklahoma City so that part was simple. Sell and split the funds. But, first, they would need to remove all the personal items in the house. That would take much time. They had already both taken so much leave of absence from their jobs. Now, they would need even more time. Maybe Jeff had ideas about who to call to help them.

When they got to Dallas, they both needed to go by their apartments, and get some different clothes to take with them for the task. They had been living out of the same clothes in the suitcases for a while now. That took a little while. Then, they were back on the road again. It was getting dark but they needed to drive on to their destination. They had both decided to stay at the house. They would just need to stop, and get groceries.

They arrived at the house with a few necessary groceries, found the house untouched, and with the plants half dead from lack of care, but, otherwise, nothing had changed. They immediately went to the bureau, opened the drawer, and did find a life insurance policy on their dad, a whole life policy that was paid up. That would be a big help for all they needed to have done. They would show the policy to Jeff Willingham, and have him direct them on how to get payment. After eating some dinner, they went to their rooms, and fell asleep.

Chapter 87:
A Meeting of the Minds

Back in Jeffersonville at the Police Station, the chief arranged a meeting with ICE, and the local FBI office, to discuss how to proceed with the case. Detective Chestnut filled them in on all the details of how everything came about, all the people involved, and the possible link to a deported individual with knowledge of a Mexican crime boss. It all seemed incredible but, to the agents, not so much. They took lots of notes, promised to check things out on their end, and get back with the chief and Detective Chestnut. They also wanted to interview Chef Marta and the detective asked that she be present during that process. They hesitantly agreed, and asked her to set the meeting up at the police station on December 27th.

Detective Chestnut then knew she had to let Chef Marta know about the scheduled meeting, along with who would be there, and why. She called, and asked Gustav to have Marta call her as soon as possible.

When Chef Marta called, she was nervous as she was anticipating a call regarding Alejandro's death. When she heard that ICE and the FBI were involved, she was *really* nervous, and knew then that it involved her husband. She was dreading the meeting, but knew in her heart it had to happen so she agreed.

Chapter 88:
Jeff Willingham

Attorney Jeff Willingham heard from the two brothers the next morning, and searched his calendar to make time for them. He found an opening and he asked them to come to Live Well Pharmaceuticals as he was conducting final interviews for the CEO position that day as well.

When they arrived, they filled him in on the news about the death of their dad and the death of the person responsible for their mother's death, and showed him the life insurance policy. Then, they just needed him to tell them exactly what to do, starting with their dad's body.

Jeff was completely shocked at the turn of events, and felt incredibly sorry for those two young men, facing all of that at that time in their lives. He tried to gather his thoughts as to what to do first. First, contact the warden at the federal prison. Second, contact the life insurance company. Third, get death certificates for both Harold and Renata Castleberry. Then, and only then, could they start the probate process. He also asked the boys if they had found any other papers in the bureau. Sadly, they had not. It would be probate with heirship proceedings, which would take longer, and be much more expensive to file. But, that would be the route they needed to take. He gave the young men the forms he needed filled out to get started. Then, he proceeded to make those needed calls.

They then left, went to the house to take a basic inventory of what was there, and made a list of what they needed to do. They certainly needed help. They were directed to a company that helps seniors move. They placed a call to the company, and asked for a person to come out and give them an estimate, both

time-wise and, of course, bottom line. Then, they would know **what** they were facing.

Chapter 89:
Chef Marta's Dilemma

When Detective Chestnut told Chef Marta about Alejandro's death, she was surprised at her reaction. She halfway expected her to be relieved, but not to start sobbing. Then her repeating, "so much death," over and over made no sense. Now that there was yet another death to investigate, she really needed to speak with Marta again but, since I.C.E. and the FBI were involved, Marta would also be interviewed by them. They agreed to let the detective be in the interview room but she was to let them handle the questions.

When Chef Marta was on her way to the police station, she was nervous, and prayed that she would do nothing that would result in harm to her husband. Deep down, she hoped he had nothing to do with the situation but was she certain?

When she entered the station, she was greeted by Detective Chestnut, who assured her she would be in the room with her. That did make her feel somewhat better but still worried. They were brought into a room with three others already there. They introduced themselves to her as Agent Jones from I.C.E., Agent Bolivar from the FBI, and Chief of Police Rogers. They told her the interview was being recorded, which was standard procedure in investigations.

The questions started off with asking her name, her address, where she was employed, for how long, and what her duties were. Then, they asked about her family members. Who was living with her? She told them about her mom and her two teenagers. Then, the questions started about what happened at the senior living community, the investigation, her shielding her husband, and his being deported. She answered all of them truthfully and they were completely satisfied.

Then came the questions she was dreading. Where was her husband now? When was the last time she saw him, or heard from him? What does he do in Mexico? She answered all but one of them easily. She faltered when they again asked the question, "When was the last time you saw him?"

She broke down, and started crying. Detective Chestnut asked if they could take a break. She got Marta some tissues and water. When Marta had composed herself, she answered honestly, "When I arrived home from The Mistletoe Inn on Christmas Day, my husband was there with my mom and our kids. It was a total surprise to me. Of course, I was happy to see him, but was worried as well. He said not to worry, that he couldn't stay long because he rode with someone else who had business here."

Then, the questions really got hard. Agent Bolivar asked, "Who did he ride with?"

Chef Marta answered, "He did not say, just that there was nothing for me to worry about."

Agent Bolivar responded, "What kind of business was he referring to? Killing someone?"

Chef Marta just dabbed at her eyes, and did not answer.

Agent Jones asked, "Was Alejandro your husband's cousin?"

Marta answered, "Yes."

Agent Jones said, "Were they close?"

Marta answered, "*No!* Alejandro was always involved in bad things so they were not close at all."

Agent Jones asked, "Who did Alejandro work for?"

Marta replied, "I do not know his name but he is a crime boss in Mexico. Alejandro has done things for them before."

"What type of things?" Agent Jones asked.

Chef Marta responded, "I am not totally sure but they were illegal. I was told by my husband always to never have anything to do with Alejandro."

Agent Bolivar asked, "But, you did see him as he came to you at your job asking for money, which apparently you had given him in the past?"

Marta answered, "Well, yes, I had given him money once a few months ago when he said he needed some money to repay someone he owed. I gave him fifty dollars, which was all I had. That was the only time. This time I refused and then he threatened my coworker. I screamed and the detective got the situation handled. That was the last time I saw him."

Chief Rogers then said, "Did you know that your husband came to visit him on Christmas Day?"

Marta was shocked, "*No!* Are you certain? Because, he was at my house for quite a while."

Chief Rogers asked, "What time did he leave?"

Marta answered, "I do not really know. I fell asleep early due to my being exhausted. When I awoke, he was gone but he left me a present on his pillow."

Chief Rogers responded, "So, he could have gone, and visited the jail while you were asleep?"

Marta sighed, and said, "I guess so."

Agent Bolivar asked, "How do you contact him?"

Marta answered, "I have a phone number to contact and he calls me back when he gets the message."

Agent Bolivar said, "We will need that number, please."

Marta reluctantly gave it to them. Then they told her that she would need to contact Detective Chestnut immediately when she heard from him again. She agrees and the Interview was over.

Chapter 90:
Gustav and Olive Learn the Truth

When Marta got back to the inn, she asked Gustav if she could speak privately to him and Olive. Of course, he agreed and they went into the office. She then told them everything about the day's questioning.

She told them about Alejandro and what he had done. She also told them what she knew about Alejandro, and his being a "foot soldier" for a Mexican crime boss. What he was doing there, she did not know or care. Then, he had been charged with manslaughter in the death of Renata, and failure to stop and render aid to her as he forced her off the road to her death.

He had been charged with those crimes, and was refused bail. But, someone had taken matters into their own hands by killing him. How? They had bound and gagged an older guard, took his uniform, locked him in a supply closet, and, as he lay there unconscious, he died, probably from a heart attack.

Then, dressed in the guard's uniform, the person entered Alejandro's cell, and stabbed him in the heart, killing him instantly. The killer made his way out of the station, never letting the camera see his face.

She added, "The agents think my husband is a suspect since he was definitely here that day. They say he visited Alejandro in jail before he came to my house, and then, after I fell asleep, he left my house, went to the jail, and murdered Alejandro."

Gustav and Olive were noticeably shocked. Gustav asked, "Do you think that is true?"

Marta answered, "*No!* My husband is no killer. Now, I am not sure of the person who gave him a ride. He would not tell me who it was or what business he had in Jeffersonville. I think he may have been sent by the crime boss to get rid of Alejandro before he could talk. Those people are ruthless and he was a loose end to them."

Marta continued, "I gave the agents the number I call to reach my husband. I just do not know what will happen now."

She started sobbing and Olive went to her, and hugged her. They both assured her they would stand with her, no matter what. Chef Marta was so happy, and told them how lucky she feels to have found such caring employers who are like family. They told her to go home, and be with her kids and her mother, and to try to relax.

When she left the inn, Gustav and Olive talked privately, and realized the situation could be very bad for her. They decided to speak with Detective Chestnut themselves, and gave her a call. When she answered, Gustav point blank asked her whether Chef Marta was in trouble.

The detective answered, "Well, she did cooperate with the FBI and I.C.E. agents so I really do not know. I think they believe her but, since she was convicted of hiding a felon, and aiding and abetting him before, I am not totally sure."

Gustav thanked her for her honesty, and promised to relay any useful information that he learned about the case. Then he hugged Olive, and promised her that everything would be alright.

He secretly hoped it would, anyway.

Chapter 91:
Hands Across the Border

It seemed the FBI had been alerted that someone was there who was on their most wanted list; a hired killer who performed jobs for notorious crime figures. They did not want to alert Marta that they had an idea of who had killed Alejandro and the guard because they wanted to see how much she knew, and how her husband could be involved. That gave them some leverage.

The FBI and I.C.E. agents devised a plan to use Marta's past conviction to lure her husband out of hiding, and, therefore, get the information they needed to apprehend the dangerous killer. They were not sure Detective Chestnut would go for the plan because it appeared she had a soft spot for Marta. They went to the Chief of Police to run it by him, and let him tell her about the plan.

The plan was to arrest her on revocation of probation due to hiding her husband yet again, which led to two murders being committed. She then would be given her one phone call and, obviously, it would be to her husband. Then, they suspected that he then would probably turn himself in rather than have her spend time in jail. They would promise him immunity and a new identity for the information unless he pled guilty, which also would reveal the killer, who was more than likely sent to get rid of Alejandro.

They met with the Chief of Police, who agreed to go over the plan with Detective Chestnut, and set it in motion. Meanwhile, operatives in Mexico were busy trying to track down who Alejandro was working for. They used the number Marta gave them to narrow down the whereabouts of the organization, and her husband. Extradition could be a long process so they preferred to bring them to the U.S. to be arrested.

Detective Chestnut did not like the plan, but clearly did not have much choice as she and Gary set out to arrest Marta. As they arrived at her home, they saw her mother and the teens. They felt so sad for doing that part of the process, seeing how much her family depended on her. Everyone was crying as they took her away. Detective Chestnut was secretly praying that the plan would work quickly, and would not lead to any more deaths.

They arrived at the police station and Marta was finger printed, booked, and given one phone call. As expected, she called the phone number in Mexico, and let the person know what had just happened. They were to give the message to her husband as soon as possible. He would know what to do, hopefully, as Marta feared for his safety.

When the news reached Juan, he thought long and hard about what to do. He had to be smart, and not involve too many people. The agents wanted him for the murders, and were trying to lure him out of hiding. Of that he was certain. But, how could he let his wife suffer for him? She had already done so once. He just could not let her spend time in jail. Alejandro had it coming and he was sorry the guard had to pay the price but that was just how it was.

Juan decided to ask the one person he trusted most in Mexico. He would know what to do.

Chapter 92:
Juan's plan

Juan met with his long-time friend, and trusted confidant, Henry Ortega. Henry was a well to do business man who had many interests in Mexico, as well as in Texas. He conducted business legally, but was very well connected with people who could help you out of a situation there, as well as in Texas. Henry told Juan not to worry. He would be in touch.

The next day, Henry told Juan to prepare to leave Mexico for good. He would go onboard one of Henry's trucks as a transportation worker and, if they were stopped, he would be a documented employee with a new name and ID. They were to travel to their destination of Tyler, and make their delivery. Then, another truck would take him to Jeffersonville, all with the new ID. When he arrived there, he was to turn himself in, and wait for an attorney who Henry hired. That would be the attorney for both Juan and Marta.

The attorney would take care of Marta's charge, which they were certain would go away when her husband came into the picture. Then, he would work on clearing Juan. Since Juan had told Henry everything, they had a defense plan of their own. When Juan left Henry, Henry arranged a meeting with the crime boss, a longtime acquaintance with whom he had mutual respect. Neither ever crossed the other even though Henry operated businesses legally. He did pay protection monies to the boss, as was the unspoken practice in Mexico power circles.

The meeting went well and Henry was assured a person would surface for the agents to investigate, and to pin both murders on. That would lead to the release of Juan and Marta both.

Chapter 93:
Juan and Marta Together Again

The next day, the plan worked as laid out. Juan rode in the truck to Tyler, and was then put in another truck, and transported to Jeffersonville, where he turned himself in to Detective Chestnut, who immediately called the agents. Juan's one phone call was to the attorney who met him there, and was going to be present at his interrogation by the two agents.

The attorney also asked to meet with Marta, asked for her to be released, and agreed to represent her. After meeting with him, Marta was surprised, but hopeful, about the possibility of she and Juan being together legally again.

Detective Chestnut notified both the agents about Juan's appearance and they planned a time to meet. She then notified Juan's attorney so he could be present. She made sure that Marta knew as well.

Marta, upon her release, went straight to Gustav, and explained what had happened, and filled them in on what was to come, at least as far as she knew. They both vowed again to help her in any way they could.

Marta then went home to her family, who were very happy to see her. She told them about Juan's being in jail, and the impending meeting with the agents. The whole family prayed together for vindication for Juan, and a new start for he and Marta.

Chapter 94:
The Inquisition

The next morning, Agents Bolivar and Jones, Chief Rogers, Detective Chestnut, and Juan and his lawyer all met in the large conference room for the interrogation. First, they made sure that Juan spoke and understood English without the use of an interpreter. He and his attorney both reassured them he did. Then, for the record, he told them his name, and how he was deported in the first place.

Then the questions got harder. They asked about Alejandro and his relationship to Juan. No problem there, until they asked how close they were. Juan honestly told them they were not close since Alejandro went to work for a notorious crime family in Mexico, and committed many crimes.

Agent Bolivar asked, "Did you know that Alejandro had been trying to extort money from your wife, Marta?"

Juan answered, "Only after she telephoned me, and told me about it."

Agent Bolivar continued, "That was not the first time. She did give him money once before. Are you aware of that?"

Juan answered "Yes, but only a little. He said he needed it to repay someone, or something like that. She believed him at the time. When she told me about it later, I told her never again. Do not believe him because he is a criminal."

Then, agent Jones intervened, "Who did he work for?"

Juan's attorney intervened, and said, "No comment for fear of retribution."

Agent Jones continued, "So you are prepared to be tried for the two murders here, Alejandro and the guard who was killed as well?"

Juan's attorney continued, "My client is innocent of these charges and we will prove this beyond a reasonable doubt."

Agent Bolivar asked, "How did you arrive here on Christmas Day?"

Juan answered, "I rode with someone, hiding in the back seat underneath some blankets. We drove at night, and were never stopped."

Agent Bolivar then asked, "Who was this driver?"

Juan answered, "I do not know his real name. I was told to call him Sir, and not ask any questions in return for access to Alejandro."

Agent Bolivar continued, "So, what did you do when you arrived?"

Juan replied, "I visited him here during visiting hours. Then, he dropped me off at our house to see my kids and my wife. He told me he would contact me when it was time to go. I stayed at the house until he contacted me. We again left at night, and drove back to Mexico."

Agent Bolivar responded, "So, you did not know Alejandro was dead?"

Juan answered, "I did not ask any questions of him, and only spoke when he spoke to me. That was our deal."

Agent Bolivar added, "This sounds way too convenient for me. How about you, Agent Jones?"

Juan's attorney said, "Are there any more questions? If not, my client is tired, and needs to rest."

At that, the interview was concluded and Juan was escorted to his holding cell, awaiting any charges levied against him.

The two agents, the chief and the detective were all sharing their thoughts on Juan and what they should do next. Detective Chestnut interjected that Juan seemed to answer everything completely. Surely, they understood his reluctance to give them the name of Alejandro's boss. Look what happened to him! They, obviously, could not assure him of protection from a hitman. The police chief took offense at that statement, and said that, on Christmas Day, there was an alternative crew of guards working and it was highly unfortunate but they would be ready if it were to happen again. The agents almost laughed at that statement.

Chapter 95:
New Year's Eve

New Year's Eve dawned cold and cloudy. The Mistletoe Inn was hosting a party for the townspeople who wanted to celebrate together with music, great food, and a lovely location. Chef Marta, who had been released from jail, was pulling out all the stops to provide some treats to ring in the new year memorably. She worked all day on them in preparation for a great party. When it came time for the party to begin, she was trying to carve out some time to visit Juan in jail. Just as people were arriving, she snuck out the back door for a quick visit with Juan before the party was really in full swing. She did tell Bambi Lynn where she was headed.

Gustav, Olive, and Jackson were greeting the guests and Bambi Lynn was making sure everyone had everything they needed. Detective Chestnut and Gary were invited, though hesitant to appear if there was to be trouble at the jail. Bambi Lynn was certainly hoping they would be there so she and Gary could perhaps share another kiss.

Chef Marta dashed over to the jail, and was just about to visit Juan when she ran into Detective Chestnut. The detective asked her about the party and she said she was going right back after her visit with Juan. Detective Chestnut had Gary bring Juan into the visitation room, and then went back to her office. She could not help but feel something was about to happen. What, she did not know. But, something…

While they were visiting, a call came in about an unresponsive person found in a vehicle in front of the courthouse. When deputies arrived, they found a male deceased in the driver's seat of a car that had been reported stolen. The coroner was called and the investigation began. She and Gary went to see the deceased, and noticed a needle mark on his arm. They also found a syringe in the car, and bagged it for forensics to check. It was an apparent overdose. The victim had not been dead long and no note was found. In checking the body, there was a wallet with an ID card from Mexico.

When the body was released to the coroner, and the forensics team was busy examining the car, and dusting it for prints, Detective Chestnut and Gary both felt they could safely slip away, and go to the New Year's Eve party for a bit.

By the time they arrived, Chef Marta was back, and serving all her wonderful party food to the many guests. Gary went immediately to see Bambi Lynn, who was very happy indeed to see him.

The party was in full swing with music from a local DJ, who never failed to get people out on the dance floor.

It was proving to be quite the night. What a great ending to the year; a year of many challenges, but also many triumphs. Gustav could not have been any happier and who could blame him? While he had once worried about bankruptcy, the inn had definitely recovered, and was *the* spot for events for the entire town, not to mention the out of town guests.

As the guests were being wined and dined, Gary finally got Bambi Lynn all to himself, and had located a mistletoe leaf. He held it over his head and they shared a kiss, signaling their happiness at finding each other. What would the new year bring? They were excited at the possibility.

As the night wore on, Detective Chestnut made her exit, leaving Gary to enjoy himself. She wanted to check on things at the police station one more time before she went home. As she arrived, she decided to visit with the coroner, and see if any progress had been made on the deceased male. She was told it was definitely looking like an overdose but they were awaiting the toxicology results.

On a whim, she decided to let Agents Bolivar and Jones know the deceased male was a Mexican National just in case they might want to be involved. She had to leave messages for both men, but felt assured they would want to check out the person themselves on the odd chance that he might be involved in the Alejandro case.

As she drove home, she was remarking on the turn of events that led her to The Mistletoe Inn during the past month, and how the chain of events spiraled from the a simple mistletoe plant, humble in appearance, but oh so deadly.

Epilogue

January 15, trial day. Scarlett Johnson finally gets her day in court. Her attorney, Robert Blake, had completely built a defense showing every other possible suspect with as much or greater motive and opportunity than Scarlett.

In his opening statement, he detailed the accident that took the lives of Scarlett's parents and ruined her childhood. He talked about how Mr. Fathom was only given a slap on the wrist. He never apologized or accepted responsibility for his crime. He paid for her schooling which, in his mind, was very generous, but, in actuality, was blood money to her.

The jurors heard statements from the other guests at The Mistletoe Inn during that time, they saw diagrams of the Inn and heard from the Detective and her assistant Gary.

The Prosecutor did bring to the jury the mortar and pestle set that had been found in her room with residue in it. The Defense countered that with reminding the jury that Scarlett operated an essential oils business, selling them at farmer's markets, holiday markets, etc.

In the closing argument, Robert Blake reminded the jury that to convict her, they must find her guilty beyond a reasonable doubt and that, in his mind, that would be impossible. He asked them to find her innocent. The Prosecutor, of course, said this was an open and shut case because of her confession in front of the guests at the dinner that evening with the Detective present.

In the end, the jury found her guilty of manslaughter and gave her probation and community service.

Charles and Michael Castleberry were able to get death certificates for both their parents, with the help of Attorney Jeff Willingham to start the probate process. Then, they focused on cleaning and repairing the house so as to get it ready to sell, after the probate hearing. The hearing is scheduled for March and, by then, everything should be taken care of at the house, so the realtor can list it for sale and Charles and Michael can move on with their lives.

Gustav and Olive Boudreaux are looking forward to Valentine's Day as they have an event filled calendar for their guests. Bookings are coming in and they are very excited about the possibilities for the new year. Cameron Mathis, the travel writer, had written a stellar review for the Inn, and that, alone, had brought in many new bookings!

Chef Marta is still serving her wonderful treats at The Mistletoe Inn and her husband, Juan, was cleared of all charges, given a new Green Card, and now is looking towards applying for citizenship. This is, in no small part due to Henry's lawyer that provided great counsel to Juan.

The Mexican National that was found dead of an apparent overdose was, indeed, a "foot soldier" sacrificed by the Mexican Crime Boss to appear to the authorities as Alejandro's killer. He was a loose end that had to be dealt with anyway, so, after the meeting between the Crime Boss and Henry Ortega, it was agreed to offer him up to the I.C.E. and FBI agents.

Thank you for joining me at The Mistletoe Inn. I hope you enjoyed your stay. I hope you can join me next year for Roses, Truffles, and Revenge, set in The Pink House Bed & Breakfast, the second novel in The Texas Bed & Breakfast Series.

About the Author

Sheila Williamson is a wife to Jeff, mom to Chad, and friend to many in Mckinney, Texas. This is her first Murder Mystery and the first in the Texas Bed and Breakfast series. Sheila is an avid reader herself, with mysteries always being her favorite since she was very young.

Sheila's first book "Two Calls Blossoming Faith: Keeping Hope Alive" is their family story of a tragic accident, subsequent drug addiction, homelessness, incarceration, rehabilitation, and redemption. Sheila wrote it to help families experiencing the most unthinkable to offer them hope and resources to help them.